I0520375

The

First Lady

Wife of President James Smith

A Novel by
James J. Stewart

1.
Beginnings

Before we can talk about First Lady Lauryn Boyer Smith and her work at the White House, we need to take a look at her background. Lauryn Boyer grew up in a Christian home on the north side of Long Beach, California. After attending Mark Twain Elementary School, she attended Hoover Junior High and Lakewood High School, where she excelled in her science and math classes. Boyfriends came and went, but she did not get serious with anyone. She was valedictorian of her high school class and graduated with a 4.0 grade-point average.

With a full scholarship to California Institute of Technology, she completed her bachelor's degree in Astrophysics in three years. At the same time, she continued to be quite active in her church in Long Beach, and she loved to work in the ministry to children there. She always looked forward to Sundays.

When Lauryn Boyer first saw Jim Smith, she was not impressed. He was on the other side of the foyer of her church, talking with some teens. Yes, he was tall and handsome, but rather skinny. Dressed in a white polo shirt and denim pants, he seemed to fit in with the other men in the church. Lauryn was usually attracted to men more muscular and athletic.

At that moment, Jim Smith looked at his watch and knew he had better get up and take his place on the stage. When he was a little boy, he started playing his parents' piano before he had his first lesson. Although he now preferred playing Broadway show tunes, professionally he could play anything from J.S. Bach to the Contemporary Christian Music and everything in between. Although he enjoyed being on the concert stage periodically, Jim made most of his income writing scores for movies and television, and then he made still more money by conducting orchestras on sound stages, conducting the scores he had written. Jim was unaware of Lauryn's gaze when he turned and walked up the steps into the worship area. He was playing the electronic keyboard and acoustic piano that morning.

As the worship leader invited people to stand and sing, the church's praise team began the first song, and Lauryn found a place in the last row. She quickly realized that the new guy on the praise team was amazingly talented. Lauryn had no way of knowing about his established work in the entertainment industry. She did not recognize Jim as the wealthy man who he was, simply because he was seldom seen in any of the media. He worked behind the scenes and worked hard.

After the first praise song and leader's prayer, he introduced the new artist. "Good morning, everyone, and welcome. For those of you who do not know him, our new keyboard artist this morning is Jim Smith. I met him at the 'Y' a couple of weeks ago, and when I learned that he is an arranger and pianist, I asked him if he had a church home in the area. He had just moved into a condo in Belmont Shore, not far from here. His house in Malibu was destroyed by last month's big brush fire that was in the news. I invited him to join us on Sundays. Welcome, Jim." There was scattered applause, and then the worship service continued.

Since the keyboard artist was a professional musician, Lauryn was mildly interested. Before she graduated from high school, she had started doing some modeling. Southern California photographers loved working with her, and she made good money. She had no college student debt. She was going to graduate with her bachelor's degree in astrophysics in a few weeks.

Lauryn and Jim did not have the opportunity get acquainted beyond being briefly introduced that Sunday morning he played on the praise team. Many months later, when the church had a catered dinner on Easter Sunday after church, Lauryn and Jim were both seated at a table with several other single adults. She discovered that Jim was brilliant, and they talked animatedly. He asked her out for that same Sunday evening. Jim was a little over twice her age at the time, but Lauryn did not hesitate.

After they had dinner, Jim took Lauryn up on Signal Hill, where they could see the sparkling lights of Long Beach. As he turned off his Tesla SUV, Jim turned towards her. "Have you ever been up here?"

She nodded. "The first time was when I was a junior at Lakewood High. Do you come up here frequently?"

He shook his head. "I only moved into my condo just two weeks ago. I am still exploring the area. Ask me about places in the Hollywood or Malibu areas, and I am an expert. As soon as I started making some real money in the entertainment industry, I bought my house in Malibu." He got a wistful look on his face. "I already miss that place, but life goes on. What about you? What are you going to do after you graduate? Do you have employment lined up?"

"I got an offer from NASA, but I'm not ready to move to Texas. I am probably going to skip getting a Masters' degree and begin work immediately on my doctorate. I make enough money doing modeling to pay all my bills with a little left over. Besides, I am starting to do commercials. There's better money there. So far, I have been able to avoid doing the 'T and A' jobs by introducing and promoting technically complex products. Recently, I was hired to be the spokes model for Sony's cinematography division."

Jim smiled. "That's great! I have got friends who are cinematographers, though I don't get to see them often. Most of the people I work with in the industry are musicians. When I work on Christian movies, I cut my rates by half or more, but for other arrangements and performances, I charge all that the traffic will bear. That means I can help out my parents if they're having a bad year."

"What do your parents do?"

"They have a farm just north of Wheatland, about thirty-five miles north of Sacramento. So long as there is enough water, they do well with each year's harvests of peaches and almonds. What do your parents do?"

"Mom's a microbiologist at Scripps, and Dad's a biochemist."

As their conversation continued until past 2:00 A.M., they discovered they had a lot in common. That Sunday evening was the first of countless times together. Just over a year later, Jim knelt on one knee at Tunnel View in Yosemite and asked Lauryn to marry him. He gave her an engagement ring with 11 karats of diamonds.

After an engagement of five months, they had their wedding at their church in Long Beach. A chartered jet flew them to Iceland for their honeymoon. Their honeymoon included a pretty comprehensive itinerary. Their driver guide was very flexible when they asked to visit Djorolaey which on the planned schedule.

Each day, the driver also recommended extra sights, like the famous Dentifoss waterfall featured in a movie for which Jim had written the score. They visited Geysir, Eldhraun lava fields, mud pools of sulfuric acid, and bathed in Blue Lagoon. Lauryn was fascinated with Thingavellir national park, and when they visited Lake Myvatn, Jim took many pictures.

Each night they enjoyed the more intimate aspects of their honeymoon. They were unconditionally and passionately in love. Towards the end of their ten days there, they set aside a full day for a glacier tour. Their last full day they spent taking in the sights of Reykjavik. By that time, they were getting tired, but they were still blissfully happy.

The night before their flight back to Long Beach, Lauryn snuggled up next to her new husband in front of a fire in their hotel's large fireplace. "Jim, even though we spent each night in a different hotel, I think all of this has been perfect."

Jim nodded thoughtfully. "Somehow, I think God has prepared some great adventures for us, and this has only been an appetizer."

Lauryn kissed him on the cheek. "Let's find some way to get back here on one of our anniversaries, just to enjoy the northern lights. What do you think?"

Jim nudged her and smiled. "That's a date! Shall we come back before or after we have kids?"

Lauryn put her head on his shoulder. "If we have two, let's come back both before and after. If we have four, let's wait until all four are old enough to appreciate this place."

They decided that they wanted as many children God seemed to want them to have. During their first ten years of marriage, they had four children, including two girls and two boys. Their oldest, a boy they named Tony, was born ten months after they returned from their honeymoon. Their oldest girl, Claudia, was born almost two years later. Claudia's younger sister, Brittany, was born when Claudia was just past her second birthday. The youngest in the family, Zack, was born almost three years after Brittany.

Those early years of her romance and marriage, Lauryn continued to be a spokes model for various products. She published a well-received collegiate-level textbook on astrophysics. She also wrote a very profitable book called *Physics for Everyone*. Jim won two Oscars for movie scores he wrote, and he won four Emmys for his music work in television. The more successful people in the entertainment industry knew that both Lauryn and Jim were politically non-partisan, and that they did not like discussing politics.

On one occasion, a director who should have known better tried to press Jim into discussing a red-hot issue for the industry. Jim and Lauryn took turns attacking and poking fun at the logic of both sides of the debate. They got the director laughing so hard he gave up trying to defend himself.

Lauryn and Jim realized that satire was a special source of fun for them, particularly when they took care to be playful and not mean-spirited. As their four children were all in school by then, the couple began to satirize almost everything in the news in their blogs.

Shortly after their sixteenth anniversary, their lives began to take an unexpected turn. Lauryn was getting ready to grill hamburgers for the family one warm summer evening when Jim came home from conducting an orchestra on a sound stage all day. Lauryn turned away from the grill for a hug and a kiss. "Hey, handsome, did you finish up the soundtrack?"

"Yep. I also got a phone call from the chairman of the inauguration committee for the Democratic Party. They are assuming a win, and they want me to put together an orchestra. At the ceremony, they want movie soundtrack selections, and they also want the same orchestra to play for one of the inaugural balls. That inaugural committee chairman talks a mile a minute. His name is Chuck Maverick. He did not even flinch when I told him that each musician would have to have a thousand-dollar advance before September 1, and that I have to have twenty-five thousand before that same day. I told him that the advances were non-refundable. He said 'fine.'"

Lauryn grinned. "So, you'll be performing for the Democrats this year, huh?"

"I don't see why not. If the Republicans called me, I would have given them the same rates."

As their family of six was eating, Lauryn also had news. "This morning, I got a call from Jack Fisher, the man from Sony that originally set up the commercial I did last March. Sony wants me to do five more commercials for their smart phones over the next year. We will have to pray about it before we go to bed tonight. Kids, if you're finished eating, you can put your dishes in the dishwasher, and you're excused."

There was a chorus of "Thanks, Mom," as they got up and left the table.

"Jim, you and I both like our phones from Sony, so if God gives us the go-ahead, I think this'll be a good fit."

He nodded. "In retrospect, I think I should have prayed with you about doing the inaugural music. It's going to be interesting to see what develops over the next couple of months. I'll start recruiting musicians tomorrow."

While Jim recruited musicians over the following three weeks, Lauryn finalized arrangements with Sony and made her second commercial. Her actual work on the set took four days. She stayed in a hotel in Hollywood while Jim stayed with the kids at their home in Long Beach. On the following Saturday, they celebrated finishing her job with a trip to Disneyland for the whole family.

Most of the news began to focus upon the coming presidential election. All but their youngest boy stayed up to watch the election results on November 8th. It was an upset. Although the early results seemed to indicate that the Democrats would win, the family could see by 9:00 PM that the Republicans had it sewn up. Lauryn looked around their family room. "Okay, kids, the election is basically over, and tomorrow you need to get up at your usual time to go to school."

"Ah, Mom!"

Jim smiled. "You heard your Mom! Off to bed!"

As the kids were getting up and going, Jim nudged her and spoke quietly. "The dishes are all done, so all we need to do is lock up. This will give us more time for you and me. How about spending some time in the whirlpool?"

"Right!" Lauryn headed upstairs to help the kids get to bed as quickly as possible. She had insisted that they all take their showers and brush their teeth before they started watching the election results unfold. Now she looked forward to making out with Jim in their whirlpool tub. It did not take Jim long to check to see that the doors were locked, and he set the security system.

In bed an hour later, they were continuing to chat after they turned off the lights. "Jim, do you think the Democrat inaugural committee will try to get their deposit back?"

"I don't know. They can try, but I have a copy of the notarized agreement. If they push it, our lawyer can handle it. When are you going to do another commercial for Sony?"

"The preparations have already started. I doubt I'll be on a sound-stage before late February."

"It's amazing how much goes into thirty seconds or a minute of airtime."

"I understand this one's going to be a full minute, with a twenty-second cut used on the Internet. They are hinting at new technology and two new phone models to be released in April. It's designed to be a teaser to create demand for the phones before they are officially announced and in full production. Shall we say good-night now?"

Saying good night took a while.

Thursday morning, Jim's phone went off just after Lauryn turned off their alarm. "Hello?"

"Good morning, Mr. Smith, this is Evan Boyer of the Republican National Committee."

Jim was suddenly fully awake. "Yes, Mr. Boyer, what can I do for you?"

"Last summer, I was unavoidably delayed in calling you, and you were signed to do inaugural music for the

Democrats. May I assume that you and your musicians have no further commitment to them?"

Jim's mouth hung open slightly for a moment. "That is correct, sir."

"Would you be interested in doing the same job, but for us Republicans?"

"My wife and I will have to pray about it. May I call you back tomorrow?"

"That being the case, I would like to have that call by noon Eastern Time, which will be 9:00 AM Pacific Time."

"I can do that, sir. Shall I call you at the number displayed on my phone?"

"That's all right, but I prefer to call you at 9:00 AM Pacific tomorrow."

"Very well, Mr. Boyer, I'll look forward to your call."

They hung up as Lauryn walked into the bedroom. "Who was that?"

"It was a man named Evan Boyer of the Republican National Committee."

Lauryn's eyes were wide. "You're kidding!" She almost shouted.

Jim shook his head. "The Republicans want me to do for them what I was going to do for the Democrats. I told him I'd pray about it with you, and he's going to call back at 9:00 AM tomorrow morning."

"Whoa!"

Jim nodded again, grinning. "Whoa is right!"

Lauryn was thoughtful. "Assuming I go with you, Larry and Joan Platt can keep the kids at their house like they did that time last year."

"True." Jim paused, thinking. "On the other hand, we could make it a short family vacation where we see some of the sights of our nation's capital."

She nodded enthusiastically. "We'll pray it through."

"Right."

Late that night, both of them were excited when they realized that they were going as a family. They could hardly sleep. They talked about it again and again throughout the night. The next morning, Lauryn printed out notes to their children's teachers, telling them when their children would be gone and why. Jim took calls from the local newspaper and some other media outlets wanting details of the story.

January 20 was a Thursday that year. They flew out of the Long Beach airport on the Monday before, giving them three days to tour the city. Thursday morning, Lauryn and the children toured the White House while Jim and the musicians got set up and rehearsed for the ball. Their Republican hosts paid all of their expenses and saw to their every need. Lauryn and the children were thrilled, but Jim was preoccupied.

Lauryn and the children had passes to get into all of the events of Inauguration Day. They had excellent seats at the swearing in, and the whole afternoon seemed magical to the kids. Lauryn wanted the kids to see, at least briefly, all the men and women in formal attire in the White House ballroom. They were standing only a few feet from Jim when the new President made his entrance with his wife.

As President Stallings made his way through the crowd, and while people were applauding, he ended up near the bandstand. He looked at Jim and smiled. After greeting Jim by name, the President and First Lady, Tonia, greeted Lauryn and each of the children by name and chatted with them. Then, the President and First Lady began to dance.

Some other children there in the ballroom approached Lauryn and Jim's children. The youngest just talked at first, but the girls were asked by a couple of the boys to dance. Taking that cue, their boys asked other girls to dance. When Lauryn was approached by California's Senator, Paul Wilson, she accepted.

After nearly an hour passed, Jim announced a break for the orchestra and joined Lauryn and their kids. Senator

Wilson was still nearby, along with two Congressmen. Senator Wilson asked an anticipated question. "Mr. Smith, how long have you and your wife been Republicans?" Lauryn looked at her husband and winked.

They responded as they had rehearsed before they had left California at the beginning of the week. The two of them satirized Washington politics and made brilliantly astute observations about world events. They lampooned Senator Wilson and the Republicans, and then they caricatured the Democrats as well. They had everyone around them howling with laughter before Jim's break was over.

He went back to conducting the orchestra. Jim and the other musicians did a variety of music over the next several hours. Lauryn took the kids back to the hotel after about an hour, as the dancing continued.

Jim crawled, exhausted, into bed with his beautiful wife at shortly after 2:00 AM. Lauryn did not wake up when he kissed her, and then he fell back onto his pillow. After breakfast in their room on Friday morning, the family used taxis to take in some of the sights they had not seen earlier. They all were tired but happy, though Jim was still exhausted and sleepy. After dinner that evening in their room, they decided to watch the news of the day.

Something seemed a little strange as they watched. The media seemed fixated on the fact that President Stallings had greeted their family as he did. There were little features about Lauryn as a representative for Sony. They also had features about Jim and his music work with movies and television. Lauryn and Jim's kids thought that it was cool. Lauryn and Jim were simply surprised.

Their flight home on Saturday was uneventful and relaxing. When they touched down in Long Beach, there were cameras and microphones of the media waiting for them. It took them twice as long as expected to get to their car and head for home.

Both Lauryn and Jim wondered what it all might mean. Their four children were all dog-tired, and they did not need much encouragement to go to bed. All of them would be getting up to go to church the next morning, so the kids were told to get their showers before saying their prayers and going to sleep.

Before going to bed that night, Lauryn and Jim discussed what seemed to be developing in their lives, talking until well after 2:00 AM. They were tired, but since they were still so excited over their trip, they were not sleepy. After taking a shower, they reviewed the lesson Lauryn was going to teach in church school the next morning. Then they finally turned out the light.

2.
Developments

Their oldest boy, Tony, went back to his activities as a high school senior. He drove his sister, Claudia, to school each morning. She was two years behind him. Claudia's younger sister, Brittany, was enjoying her popularity in Bancroft Middle School. Her younger brother, Zack, was beginning to get comfortable with his sixth-grade teachers.

Lauryn and Jim hardly ever let an evening go by without the whole family eating together. They talked about anything and everything. While the four kids privately admitted to each other that they were not telling their parents everything, they did not realize that their mother actually knew just about everything – sometimes knowing more than they did.

They had been back from their trip to the nation's capital for less than a month when Tony dropped what thought would be a bombshell. "Dad, I think that I want to stop taking trumpet lessons. There's so much going on in my senior year."

Jim nodded. "That's understandable. You haven't been focusing on your practicing as much as you used to."

Lauryn smiled at their son. "I was wondering when you were going to get around to this."

Tony was visibly surprised at his mother. "Really, Mom?"

"Absolutely! You're trying to decide between three scholarships, you and Abby are getting serious, and almost every weekend you've got things going on that will never happen again. With so many things demanding your attention, giving up your trumpet lessons is logical."

Brittany spoke up. "Can I have your trumpet, Tony? You know I love jazz, and I want to teach myself."

Tony laughed. "Good luck with that! I've heard you play around with a few licks, but that doesn't mean you can become a jazz trumpeter!"

She stuck her tongue out at him. "You'll see!"

They all ate silently for a few minutes, then Zack spoke quietly. "Mom, you remember my telling you about Bud Jackson?"

Lauryn nodded. "The bully? I remember your having a run-in with him back in October."

"Yeah, well he got pushy before school this morning. I had to deck him before I went on into school through security. The guard, Mr. Bentley, looked at me and nodded, but he did not say a word. Bud avoided me all day today, even though I've got him in PE and Math."

Lauryn nodded. "Last November at the PTA meeting, I talked with Bud's Mom. We both knew about what happened, and I told her that my son would react differently if Bud tried it again. She said, 'Well, boys will be boys," as though that was an excuse for Bud. I told her that if Bud tried it again, he would regret it. Thanks for backing me up, Zack." She paused. "I've baked apple pie for dessert tonight. Does everybody want some?"

At dinner the next night, Brittany had a report. "Bud approached me this morning, complaining that Zack had hit him. I told him that if he was enough of a coward to pick on girls, that I was willing to give him another lesson on how to get along with other people. He said, 'You wouldn't dare!' I told him that I could also pass the word to see to it that none of the other girls in school would have anything to do with him. He turned and walked away."

Zack smiled. "Thanks, Brit!"

"You're welcome. You're my brother, and we're family. We watch out for one another, don't we, Mom?"

Lauryn nodded. "That's right."

There are many other stories that can be told about their strong family ties. Late in the summer after Tony graduated, Sony cut a deal with Lauryn to be the official presenter of their new products at a trade show in Paris.

Lauryn was excited. "What do you think, Jim? There're plenty of people at the church that will take care of the kids if you want to come along. We can take in Paris together for a week!"

Jim grinned. "As wonderfully romantic as this sounds, it will probably be hard work for you. The last week in August?" She nodded. "Gaumont Film Company has produced a biopic on Debussy and wants me to do the score. If I go with you, I could negotiate a deal with them in person."

Lauryn nodded vigorously, smiling. "Yes! Perfect! You go to the Sony trade show with me part of the time, and I'll go with you to the Gaumont studios. When we're not working, we'll take in Paris!"

When the calendar said August, it was an unforgettable trip. They had to make stops in Salt Lake City and Amsterdam before their plane touched down in the late morning, Paris time. Sony had a limo waiting for them, and the driver got them to their hotel in time for lunch. "That was delicious!" Lauryn was enthusiastic. "Sony is sending a limo for us tomorrow morning, so this afternoon, shall we do some walking?"

Jim kissed her. "That sounds great!"

They were almost asleep on their feet when they finished dinner later that day. They went to be early and left a wake-up call.

When they arrived at the trade show the next morning, the entourage there to greet them included several Parisian politicians as well as Sony executives. During the first hour, before the doors opened for the show, the only real surprise was a visit by Pierre Debré, the Prime Minister of France. He talked with Lauryn and Jim in moderately good English for several minutes, and he stayed to remain in the audience as Lauryn made her first presentation. During her first break, he talked animatedly with Lauryn and Jim about the inauguration in Washington, asking them several questions about their politics. Lauryn and Jim were polite and kept their satire and dry senses of humor in check.

Throughout their week in Paris, everywhere they went, every day they found themselves talking with politicians who wanted to be seen with the semi-famous Americans. The media's cameras and microphones were frequently there as well.

On Friday evening after dinner, Lauryn and Jim met with the producer and director of "**Debussy**," the production of Gaumont studios. Jim had done his homework before leaving the United States, so he had only a few adjustments to make to their offer before signing the contract. Jim would fly to Paris again after Christmas to spend two weeks working with the French studio orchestra.

After they returned to Long Beach, their kids had a lot to talk about. With Tony away at college in another state, Claudia was the most talkative. "I found a French media web page, where we could watch news of Europe in French with English subtitles. You were in the news almost every night you were gone."

Tony nodded. "Yeah! I think the French Prime Minister has a crush on you Mom, but what was his thing with you, Dad?"

Claudia smiled. "Yes! What was he whispering to you about while Mom was doing her thing?"

Jim raised his eyebrows. "Somehow, I think he thought that I could explain American politics to him."

"Could you?" Claudia was eating rapidly as she stayed focused on her Dad.

"Evidently, he was wanting to hear my take on things in our country because I'm established as non-partisan."

Between bites, Claudia had a steady stream of questions for her Dad, as well as for her Mom.

In January, just after Jim returned from Paris, Sony flew Lauryn and Jim to Sidney, Australia, for another trade show. They had miserable jet lag. The situation there was similar. They thoroughly enjoyed their week "down under." Sony executives were so used to working with Lauryn, they treated her like one of their corporate family. She was Sony's official spokesperson for a long time. Aussie politicians were even more enthusiastically receptive of them. The media there portrayed Lauryn as being able to influence Sony's prices. She could not, of course. In a similar way, the media portrayed Jim as an expert in American politics. He found that mildly amusing. In Long Beach, each night their kids would tune-in to Nine Entertainment's several web pages in order to keep up with their parents.

At the end of the week, Lauryn and Jim flew to Auckland, New Zealand, where they joined a two-week bus tour of the islands. By the time they got back to Long Beach, February was upon them.

For Lauryn and Jim's first dinner back home, Claudia did almost all the cooking, and Brittany had all the questions. "Mom, I could kind of understand why the French politicians hung around you and Dad so much. The French have kind of a different culture than we do, and there are language difficulties. The Aussies speak English! We have similar cultures! The media there are just as crazy about you and Dad as they were in France! What gives?"

Claudia put her fork down. "Yeah! Sometimes they seemed to be a little crazy in the way they treated you!"

Lauryn cocked her head a little with a wry smile. "Your Dad and I have been talking about this for the last two weeks. You're raising an interesting question though.

What do you think, Jim? Is it because Australia is a much closer ally to the United States right now than France is?"

Jim hesitated. "I'm sure that's some of it, but when the French people watch American movies, they see Americans as quite different from them, and they see us as less cultured. We are supposedly clumsier in our understanding of their culture, which they think is better. The Aussies watch American movies and see parallels in our cultures."

The conversations turned to discussing Aussie celebrities. Lauryn and Jim were a bit surprised when Zack spoke up. "I think Mallrat is fascinating. She's really sexy too."

There was total silence for a moment. Finally, Lauryn caught her breath and nodded. "There're a lot of fine musicians coming out of Australia. Your Dad and I didn't meet her though."

Brittany picked up on what Zack said. "Yeah, I like her music. Actors from down under seem to keep their feet on the ground pretty well. I like Josh Brolin."

As the months went by, Sony continued to use Lauryn as their spokesperson in their major markets. The biggest cultural shock came when Lauryn and Jim went to New Delhi in June, where Lauryn talked to them about Sony's new 16K movie camera. Knowing that Jim would go with her, Sony reached out to some of India's major television and film producers. After discussing Sony's new camera for their entertainment industry, then Lauryn discussed Sony's more familiar imaging products that had been released that year. That audience included several hundred people.

Most of the people they encountered in New Delhi could speak at least *some* English. Their biggest surprise came one evening after dinner when they back at their hotel. There was a knock on their door. When Jim opened the door, he was startled to see a well-dressed and distinguished-looking man they met on their second day in

New Delhi. Jim vaguely recognized him but did not attempt to pronounce his name.

"Good evening, Mr. Smith. May I come in?" He turned to a man with him. "Just stay by the door, please."

Jim nodded at their distinguished visitor. "Of course, please come in."

By this time, Lauryn was standing beside Jim, and she recognized him too. "We're honored that you have come to visit us."

He gave a slight bow. "I'm honored that you recognize me. I have come to ask a favor of the two of you."

Jim gestured towards the conversation area of their suite. "Please come and sit down with us." When all three of them were seated, Jim continued their conversation. "You said you have come to ask a favor of us."

The man cleared his throat softly. "Yes. This past November, your country elected a new man to be your President, President Stallings. Since then, I have discovered difficulties with the diplomatic channels that I used with your previous President."

Jim was thoughtful. "I must be honest with you. We really don't know President Stallings, nor have we communicated with any of the people that are close to him."

The man nodded. "Yes. I understand." He turned to Lauryn. "It may well be that it is you, Mrs. Smith, that may be able to accomplish the favor that I wish to ask."

Lauryn was startled. They were conversing with an immensely powerful man in India's politics because he was on the staff of the Prime Minister. Lauryn looked him straight in his eyes. "What are you asking of me, sir?"

"A few days ago, you had an extended conversation with our Prime Minister's wife."

Lauryn's face lit up. "Yes! I enjoyed her very much."

He nodded. "She enjoyed talking with you as well. This brings us to the favor I am asking. The wife of President

Stallings, your country's First Lady named Tonia, went to graduate school with our Prime Minister's wife at the University of Edinburgh. I am asking you to try to communicate with your new First Lady, Tonia Stallings, and tell her that she needs to communicate with our Prime Minister's wife." He took a business card from his shirt pocket. "This is her official card. It offers your new First Lady three different ways to communicate with her."

Her mouth hanging slightly open, Lauryn reached out and accepted the card. "I'm pretty sure that, between my contacts and those of my husband, we can probably accommodate your request."

The man smiled and stood up. "Thank you, so very much. I have abundant gratitude. If there is anything I can do for you during your remaining time in India, please do not hesitate to ask." He handed Jim his business card, turned and walked to the door. He turned and bowed slightly. "It has been most pleasant to meet you." He turned, opened the door, walked out, and closed the door quietly.

Stunned, Lauryn and Jim watched him leave. "Jim, of all the weird experiences we've had together, I think this one takes the cake."

Jim nodded and took out his phone. "Paul Wilson, our Senator, has an office in Los Angeles in the Arco Towers." He paused and put away his phone. "I suspect that this may be politically sensitive, so I think I should not use my cell phone to contact him."

Lauryn nodded emphatically. "You're right. Our entire conversation with him seemed like there is political intrigue going on. I'm done with my work for Sony here. What's the latest with Bollywood?"

Jim shook his head. "I've made some friends while we have been here. The future will tell."

"Okay. We can go home a day early tomorrow morning. It's just a matter of calling the airport."

Jim picked up the hotel phone and pushed buttons, including turning on the speaker. "Is this the Concierge?"

"Yes, Mr. Smith, what may I do for you?"

"Since our work here is done, we've decided to return to our country tomorrow morning instead of the next day."

"Yes, Mr. Abrams, your Sony representative informed me that you might wish to do so. Someone has arranged for a chartered jet plane for you. I can have a taxi waiting. Please tell me what time you and Mrs. Smith would like to leave the hotel."

Lauryn's mouth was hanging open, her eyes wide. "Yes, sir. Please have a bell hop come to take our luggage and escort us at 8:00 AM."

"Yes, Mrs. Smith, I'll have a bell hop there at your room with a cart at 8:00 AM. Will there be anything else?"

Jim looked at her, nodding. "No, sir. Thank you." He pressed the speaker button again to hang up.

Lauryn sounded overwhelmed. "Wow! Wow! I wonder who arranged for the private jet?"

Jim shook his head. "We've met a couple dozen people this week that have that kind of money and a lot more. We can ask tomorrow morning, but we may not get an answer."

Jim was right. The next morning, he asked the pilot, who shook his head. "I don't know, sir. My copilot and I fly people wherever we're told to do so, and we just collect our paycheck. We will refuel in New York. The flight time from here to there is fifteen hours, but we gain nine and a half hours. It will be early afternoon. I recommend that you get off and get a good meal at La Guardia before we continue to Long Beach."

Lauryn nodded. "Okay." They got on the Gulfstream, and they took off less than five minutes later. When they got to La Guardia, they had access to a frequent-flyer lounge, and they enjoyed steak dinners. Although flight time to Long Beach was another five and a half hours, they picked up another three hours.

It was a day later back in Long Beach. Jim called Senator Paul Wilson to invite him to join them for dinner. The Senator hesitated. "Mr. Smith, I have a very full schedule. I'll put you in touch with my business manager."

"That won't do, Senator. I have a message for First Lady Tonia Stallings from a political friend of hers in India."

"Who is the friend?"

"I'm not at liberty to say, Senator. Lauryn and I just got back from spending a week in New Delhi. I think you will find the dinner conversations at our family's dinner table will be quite interesting to you. How about this evening at 6:00 PM? If you wish to bring your wife, she will also be welcome"

The Senator hesitated only a moment. "Very well, we will be there with you at 6:00. I have your address in my file."

"We'll see you later, Senator. Bye." Jim ended the call.

Senator Wilson was glad he came, and so was his wife, whose name was Dot. After he made a conference call for Lauryn and Jim with First Lady Stallings' Chief of Staff, the dinner and accompanying conversations were memorable. Those were just two beginnings. After First Lady Stallings talked to her former roommate in New Delhi the next morning, she called Lauryn and Jim to thank them for making the connection for her.

Their dinner-table conversations at their home continued to discuss India and its culture for the next few weeks. Tony was home on vacation from college with his fiancée, Abby, so that added variety to their conversations. Although their coming excursion to London did not leave for another six months, life certainly did not come to a standstill. Sony had to brief Lauryn on newer products, and Jim had to finalize arrangements to write two more movie scores and a television score for his studio contacts in London.

3.
Taking Risks

Over the next three years, Sony continued to have Lauryn appear as their spokesperson in capital cities of various countries. In each case, Jim went with her. The excursions would last one or two weeks and took place every three to four months. Wherever they went, politicians wanted to be seen with them.

In almost every family dinner table discussion, Tony (when he was home), Claudia, Brittany, and Zack talked about their schools and school friends. When Tony suggested that his brother and two sisters transfer into charter schools, there was heated discussion. Claudia had less than two years left in high school and did not want to lose her friends.

Brittany finally convinced Claudia otherwise. "Look, sis, I understand why you don't want the change, and I have been looking forward to being in the same school with you again as I was in middle school. The truth is, even if you are going to Bethany High, you can still do things with your current friends. Also, Greg is pretty serious about you, and I don't think he'll stop dating you simply because you're going to different schools."

Claudia nodded. "I guess you're right. Besides, Bethany High has a fantastic chemistry lab – much better than the one at Millikan. Bethany offers a second year of chemistry, and I think I'd really like that. If you follow me to Bethany, you'll love their planetarium if you want to get deeper into astronomy, and they do field trips to both Mount Wilson Observatory and to Palomar."

Their mother nodded. "Palomar is a terrific field trip. Maybe we can all go there sometime. Griffith Park Observatory and Planetarium are also great places to visit. We did that as a family five years ago, remember?" All three kids nodded. The following semester, all three transferred to charter schools.

Meanwhile, Lauryn and Jim began to spend more time on the Internet. Without thinking about it, they were developing friendships among the people they met on their excursions to other countries. First Lady Tonia Stallings also became a friend because of Lauryn's travels. Jim never heard from President Stallings himself, but the politicians Jim met on Lauryn's trips for Sony gradually became friends through their resulting email correspondence.

Jim was working with a studio orchestra for a film directed by Alfred Wells, when the director had lunch with him. "Jim, this score you have written for me is the best you've ever done. I wouldn't be surprised if you're at least nominated for an Oscar."

"Thanks, Al. I must admit that this time some of my inspirations came when I was in London with Lauryn."

The director chewed a sandwich and washed it down with coffee. "What happened in London?"

"One evening, Lord Stanley Harris, Archbishop of Canterbury, took Lauryn and I to the old The Odeon Leicester Square art deco theater for a screening of the classic film, *El Cid*, with music by Miklós Rózsa. When I was a child, I wanted to see all of the movies with Miklós Rózsa music scores. His music in *El Cid* gave me the inspiration for this movie."

"How many movies did Miklós Rózsa score?"

"I think IMDB lists over a hundred credits for him."

"I'll have to check him out. Julie and I are hosting a party next Saturday for a few dozen friends. Would you and Lauryn like to join us?"

Jim smiled. "I'll check with Lauryn, but it sounds like fun. I'll let you know tomorrow." Finished with their lunches, they went back to work.

That evening, Lauryn did not hesitate. "Jim! Of course! I've always wanted to meet Alfred Wells! To meet him along with his wife and some of their friends? Let's go!" She turned to their oldest daughter. "Claudia, can you and Greg hold down the fort here and babysit?""

"I think so, Mom. I wish Greg and I could go with you. You're going to a Hollywood party? Wow!"

On Saturday, Lauryn and Jim arrived at the Wells' home in Malibu just before 8:00. Over the first two hours, they shook hands with many of the industry's A-list actors, directors, and producers. Lauryn was surprised at how many famous people were admirers of Jim's work. They stayed together throughout the evening.

They did not know it, but their going to that party planted seeds for their future. In their wildest imaginings, they could not foresee what was ahead for them. Meanwhile, it was merely the first of many entertainment-industry parties they would attend.

Four months later, Lauryn and Jim went on an excursion for Sony to Cologne, Germany. It was for Photokina, which is the largest annual trade show for the photographic and imaging industries. There were no developments for Jim and his work, but they made several new friends who would be important to them in the years ahead. They did not know it at the time, however.

The weekend after they returned from Cologne, they were invited to another entertainment-industry party. This one was put on in Malibu, not a half-mile from where Jim had lived many years earlier. Their hosts were Casper Whirry and his wife, Diane. He was a well-established producer, and she primarily directed popular animated features. They were billionaires.

They greeted Lauryn and Jim as they arrived. "Welcome! We're so glad you could come." They shook hands. Casper Whirry stayed by the door to greet others who were arriving, and his wife walked with them into the living room, which was huge. Diane spoke quietly. My husband and I were at the inaugural ball in the White House. We were just a few feet away when Senator Wilson asked about your Republican roots." She smiled. "I didn't see it, but according to Casper, before responding to the Senator's question you two shared a wink."

Diane stopped walking to speak directly to Lauryn and Jim. "What followed was amazing to my husband and me. The two of you satirized Washington's politics and world events. After you lampooned Senator Wilson and the Republicans, you went on to decimate the Democrats as well. All of us around you laughed for several minutes before the orchestra's break was over. I don't think I'll ever forget it."

Lauryn smiled broadly. "Jim and I decided many years ago that our best response to posturing politicians is satire. We do it to remain non-partisan while not alienating anyone unnecessarily."

Jim nodded. "We enjoyed that evening as well, though for me, it was exhausting. I'm looking forward to getting to know you and your husband this evening, Diane. I've not scored a music he has produced, but perhaps someday I will."

Diane Whirry nodded. "I suppose that is possible, although my husband has something much bigger to discuss with you this evening. I'll let him explain it to you later."

Diane's statement left Lauryn and Jim mystified. More than two hours passed before the four of them sat down at a table behind the house next to an Olympic-size swimming pool. Both Casper and Diane had come across as relaxed and at ease throughout the evening. Casper spoke quietly. Diane told me that earlier this evening you mentioned you've never scored a movie I've produced. That's true, but I have a wild idea for both of you to consider, and I'd appreciate it if you don't respond with either yes or no for at least a week."

Lauryn nodded, and Jim spoke thoughtfully. "What's your wild idea?"

"All my life I've been a conservative Democrat, and Diane has been a liberal Republican. Our politics is woven together with our love for each other."

Diane nodded. "This has been true for forty-one years."

Lauryn was amused. "I gather that Jim's and my being non-partisan doesn't bother either of you!"

Casper roared with laughter. "Actually, we find it refreshing." His laughter subsided before he spoke again. "As you undoubtedly know, our current governor is not going to run for re-election."

Lauryn shook her head. "Jim and I never lie, so we can't be good politicians. I can never keep up with all the layers and moods of politics. My husband, on the other hand, writes 26-line orchestral scores and keeps all the different instruments coordinated in his head and under control."

Jim smiled while shaking his head. "My darling, that's a new one! I'll have to think about that metaphor!"

Casper Whirry chuckled. "Jim, I'm simply asking the two of you to consider and pray about your running for Governor of California on a strictly non-partisan basis. If you decide to say yes, you'll have backing from Diane and me, along with probably at least half of our industry in the United States represented in this crowd tonight."

Lauryn looked around. Several people were looking at them and nodding. Lauryn looked at her husband. He was as astonished as she was. Throughout the rest of the evening, people expressed their support to them. When Lauryn and Jim left at shortly after midnight, they were both in a daze.

At dinner the following evening, Lauryn pointed out the obvious to the kids. "If, on the impossible chance that we would win, it will mean moving to Sacramento, leaving behind our friends here."

The kids discussed among themselves for several minutes, but at the end, they all wanted their Dad to run.

Jim was somber. "We'll all need to pray about this extensively before a decision is made."

It was a family topic of discussion for nearly a month. Lauryn asked for prayer on their church's web page, and the news spread fast. When they told Casper and Diane 'yes,' Casper had already circulated a petition to get Jim on the ballot. The state requirement was 7,000 signatures, but in just under a month, 41,000 signatures had been collected.

During the campaign, any time another candidate mentioned Jim Smith, he responded with appropriate seriousness, and then he would sometimes add a satirical but fun comment. In November, Jim won 71% of the votes, and the family moved to Sacramento.

Lauryn committed herself to manage the family's move to Sacramento, while Jim focused upon being the newly elected governor.

Over the next three years, Lauryn and Jim rebuild the state's infrastructure and improve both the state's economy and its ecology. During that first winter, Jim organized a town-hall meeting primarily of vintners, farmers, and ranchers because agriculture is the state's dominant industry. Jim listened for more than two hours as suggestions were made for how the state government can help agriculture overall.

There was extensive discussion among farmers about weed control. When Jim asked about the state employing goats for weed and brush control to reduce the impact of brush and forest fires, most of them were supportive.

Also discussed was the California State Water Project. Many of the farmers and ranchers felt that it needed to be upgraded as well as better maintained. Others pointed out the unbuilt and proposed features they thought were needed, including covering and/or enclosing the canals.

During those governor years, Lauryn frequently was the speaker for both fundraisers and for luncheons that dealt with women's issues. Meanwhile, U.S. Senator Paul Wilson announced that he was running for re-election, but as a non-partisan. Both Lauryn and Jim helped him with fundraisers, and he won easily.

During the summer of their third year in Sacramento, Jim was asked for the first time if he was going to run again. Jim said he did not know, but would announce, one way or the other, before Labor Day. The next morning, Jim got a call from Casper Whirry. "Good morning, Jim, this is Casper."

"Good morning, Casper! Are you calling because of my press conference yesterday?"

"That's right. If you run for re-election, you'll have the same supporters, but I'm wondering if you're aware of a movement beyond our home state."

"A movement? What do you mean?"

"It's something that has developed because of the Internet. Think back, Jim. Before you were elected Governor of California, you and Lauryn traveled to cities in a couple dozen countries on behalf of Sony. You did the musical scores for movies made in several countries outside the United States, and according to IMDB, you have composed the musical scores for fifty-three movies made here in the United States."

I'm aware of this Casper, but has it all to do with the movement you mentioned?"

"You and Lauryn are a popular topic of discussion in the media and on the Internet in all fifty states, as well as in dozens of other countries. Your honest politics, your sense of humor, and your music crosses all boundaries of ethnicity, religion, music genre, and politics. Does Lauryn realize that she is the most widely recognized spokesperson of all businesses?"

"I haven't really had time to ponder that, Casper."

"Maybe you should discuss it over dinner with your family, Jim. If you decide this summer to run for President of the United States, you'll get many times the support you got when you ran for Governor of California."

As Jim and Casper were talking, Jim was looking out his office window at Sacramento. Now, he had to sit down at his desk."

"Casper, this sounds even more impossible than running for Governor ever did."

"Maybe so, Jim, but Diane and I think that you and Lauryn need to pray seriously about it." Jim was silent, and Casper waited for him to say something. "Jim? Are you still there?"

Jim swallowed hard. "Yes, my friend, I'm still here." He paused. "Casper, we need to commission a reliable and non-partisan poll that explores the question before I can even seriously consider this."

"Some of the media outlets have already done it. I'll email you those results. Meanwhile, are you going to Houston for the Populist Politics Assembly in two weeks?

"Yes. I was asked three weeks ago to be one of the keynote speakers. Lauryn is speaking on Friday evening after Paul Wilson's opening address. I think I'm scheduled to speak early on Sunday morning after breakfast, after some have left to go to church services."

"Good. Okay, my friend. We'll talk more in a few days."

"Right." Casper ended the call.

The next two weeks passed all too quickly. Both Lauryn and Jim had to prepare their addresses for the assembly in Houston. Lauryn spent a weekend in Long Beach as Matron of Honor for the wedding of two church friends there. Jim's Lieutenant Governor, Bud McFall, notified the Republican party that he will run as a non-partisan for re-election.

Friday's flight to Houston was uneventful, with Lauryn and Jim relaxed and looking forward to the respite. After checking in to the Hotel Granduca, they relaxed for a while. "I've got my presentation ready for this evening, Jim. We can go downstairs and go for a swim. What do you think?"

He was thoughtful. "I suppose we could." He looked at his watch. It's early afternoon out at home, and I'm hungry. We've not had Texas BBQ for ages. Does that appeal to you?"

Lauryn's eyes got big. "Yes! That sounds great. Room service could accommodate us, but I'd rather go to the dining room."

He stood up, smiling. "Let's go!" Lauryn and Jim filled up on sausage and ribs, and when they returned to their room, they slept for two hours. They shared a chef's salad in their room before changing clothes and going to the ballroom. Their friend, Senator Paul Wilson led off the evening. As an experienced politician, Paul certainly knew how to work and audience. He got two standing ovations before concluding by introducing Lauryn. "Our next speaker is a dear friend. In my first real conversation with her, I made the mistake of asking her how long she and her husband had been Republications. She and her husband proceeded to roast me in such a nice way, I laughed until my sides ached. She's a fascinating woman, and my wife loves her dearly too. Ladies and gentlemen, Lauryn Boyer Smith!"

As he stepped away from the podium, he had another standing ovation. After a second bow, he sat down with his wife as Lauryn went to the podium. "Thank you, Paul. To this day, my husband and I seldom think of ourselves as politicians. Years ago, right after I became a spokesperson for Sony, when Jim and I went to presentation complex in Paris, for some reason there were many politicians who wanted to be seen with us. That was the beginning of having friends in other countries."

She took a sip of bottled water that she had taken to the podium. "I accepted those kinds of encounters as part of my representing Sony. Jim used those same trips to finalize details for movie scores he would write for productions made in those countries."

She took a deep breath, sighed, and relaxed. "The first time Jim and I became more deeply involved in politics, it was a total surprise. We were in a country where we often needed translators available to us. A high-ranking politician came to our hotel room to ask us a favor. As a result, when we got home, we asked Paul Wilson to help us make an international connection between two First Ladies."

This evening, I would like to talk with you about the powerful roles of women who work in the background of the political arena in many countries." Lauryn's presentation lasted more than an hour, and she was very well received. The session ended shortly before 11:00 PM.

On Saturday, the morning was filled with a variety of workshops, but in the afternoon, there were two more speakers for the general session. The first to speak after lunch was Laura Craver, who was a prominent and influential Democratic Congresswoman until the previous year in Washington State, when she became non-partisan. She ran for the U.S. Senate in the previous election and won. She spoke about navigating the conflicting political currents in her state.

In the evening after dinner, and the speaker was an African American named David Cole. For more than thirty years, he was active in the Democratic Party in New Orleans even while being the pastor of a large African American Episcopal church there. One of the things he said was, "Over the years, I got increasingly tired of the condescending attitude of the leaders of my party, perpetually reminding me how dependent people of color are, so we had to vote the straight Democratic ticket in every election. With God's help, I finally woke up. Now, I'm a non-partisan Congressman who steers clear of the Congressional Black Caucus. I'm free at last!" He got several standing ovations during his speech.

The Sunday morning schedule called for a breakfast buffet from 7:00 until 9:00, followed by Paul Wilson's introduction of the governor. Jim Smith's closing presentation would last about an hour, and Casper Whirry would close the assembly at approximately 10:00 AM. There would still be time for many to go to church.

When Jim was introduced as California's Governor, he got a standing ovation. Jim had decided to keep it light, with good-natured satire of all partisan politics. Lauryn helped him write the speech. At the end, he announced he would decide by the end of the month on re-election.

The applause lasted several minutes. Then Casper Whirry got the audience to quiet down so that he could bring things to a close. "Jim, four years ago I got you into running for governor, and I don't regret that for a moment." There was applause, but Casper indicated quiet. "I would prefer that you run for President of the United States this time. What do all of you say?" The applause was deafening.

4.
Cliff Jumping

Back at the hotel, Lauryn and Jim spent a long time on their knees, praying. When they got up, Lauryn was thoughtful. "Jim, I'm thinking about a scene in the old television series, *The West Wing*."

"Didn't we binge-watch that with the kids several years ago?"

She smiled. "Yes. Late in the series, the Chief of Staff had a heart attack, and though he survived, he had to be replaced. In the scene, President Bartlett takes his press secretary, CJ Craig, aside. The scene goes like this:

> *President Bartlett*: CJ, there's something I need you to do for me.
> *CJ*: What's that?
> *President Bartlett*: Jump off a cliff.

Jim kissed her. "Lauryn, shall we jump off this cliff together?"

She smiled broadly. "Absolutely! You betcha, Mr. President! You'd better call Diane and Casper! I think we'll be their biggest investment ever."

"I love you!" He kissed her, and then he took out his phone and dialed. "Why don't you call home?"

"Right!"

While they were flying from Houston back to Sacramento, the media and the Internet were spreading the news. The media didn't get as far as the gate in Sacramento because of security restrictions, but a stranger did meet them just inside the terminal at the gate and showed them a badge. "Excuse me, Mr. & Mrs. Smith. I'm Phil Kaiser. I'm with the Secret Service. We understand you've decided to run for President, Mr. Smith, so you and your family now have our protection. There're some things to talk about. I need to escort you to a place that's more private here in the terminal where we can talk."

That conversation delayed them before they had to face the media outside the secured part of the terminal. They were not ready to answer questions yet. For their ride back to the governor's mansion, they were in an armored SUV.

Back at home, Tony, Abby, Claudia, Greg, Brittany, and Zack were all there. Zack was possibly even more excited than Lauryn and Jim. "This so cool!" was the first thing he said.

His Dad laughed. "You might not think so a few months from now."

Lauryn was also smiling. "That's right. Outside these walls right now, there are Secret Service agents, and they will be using the guest room here in the mansion at least part of the time."

Around the dinner table that evening, they discussed Jim's resigning as governor, moving out of the Governor's Mansion before the Lieutenant Governor moved in, and the lives they would lead during the campaign. They talked briefly about what they might do if they lost the election, and then they talked about moving to Washington, D.C. It was late when they all went to bed.

While Lauryn and Jim were having their first cups of coffee the next morning, Jim's phone rang. "Good morning! This is Paul."

Jim pressed the speaker button. "Good morning, Paul."

"I wanted to call you early because Tom Striker, your campaign manager for your governorship, shouldn't do your campaign for President. It's too big for him, in my opinion."

"Lauryn and I were talking about that as we were flying home yesterday. Do you have a recommendation?"

"When I was a Republican, there were two I might have recommended, but now there's only one."

Lauryn got into the conversation at this point. "Who do you recommend, Paul?"

"Adam Paxton is the absolute best choice because he always focuses on the candidate's agenda, regardless of politics. I called him, and he's expecting to hear from you today. At the moment, he's on vacation with his wife at Lake Tahoe. Her name is Ann. He can meet with you this evening if you say so."

Jim looked at Lauryn, who both shrugged and nodded. "Lauryn and I trust your judgment, Paul, so if they can be here by 6:00 this evening, tell him he and his wife will have an excellent dinner with us and our family."

"Okay. I'll call you if he won't be there this evening. Keep me posted from now on, okay?"

"Right." Jim hung up the phone, and they stood up. "Since you've already got bacon in the oven, I'll go make sure everyone else is up. Don't forget, Phil Kaiser is briefing all of us at 9:00. Brittany and Zack will probably meet their security details too."

"This campaign may be hard on them, Jim. We're going to have to be extra patient. Right now, I'll start whipping up some pancakes."

That was the beginning of a long day. Working out routines with the Secret Service took up much of the morning. It was almost noon when Jim got to his office. His Lieutenant Governor was there to meet him. Bud McFall was a conservative democrat, and Jim both liked and trusted him. "Good morning, Bud! You and I have a lot to talk about. Shall we have lunch brought in?"

Bud nodded. "I hoped you'd suggest that, so I told my secretary that I'd call her if we didn't want burgers and fries."

"Okay, that sounds fine. Let's sit down and talk about where we go from here."

They talked most of the afternoon. Jim trusted Bud, and he knew that when Bud took over, there would be no disturbances in the state's routines. Jim would turn the reins over to Bud at the end of the month.

That evening, Lauryn and Jim immediately liked Adam Paxton. Ann, his wife, was practically adopted by Brittany and Zack, who wanted to talk to her about their new Secret Service details. Lauryn and Ann found that they had a lot in common.

The following Friday, the campaign's plane touched down in Sacramento, and less than an hour later, it took off for Iowa. Aboard the plane, in addition to Lauryn and Jim, were their initial campaign staff members and a dozen media representatives.

In the Iowa caucuses, the topics most frequently discussed were health care, education, and the national debt. Lauryn and Jim listened to each person they encountered, responding as they had discussed together during preparations

In New Hampshire, those same topics came up, but there were also frequent questions about term limits. Still others wanted to return to the original system of paying legislators per diem plus expenses, with their retirement coming from Social Security. Along the same line, in a statewide poll, 81% believed that Congress should not be able to pass laws from which they are exempt.

Lauryn returned to Sacramento during the last week of the month to coordinate moving out of the Governor's Mansion into a large home in the River Park area. Jim flew home to join her when he officially turned the governorship over to Bud McFall. That night, the whole family was there in their new home for dinner, including Tony, Abby, Claudia, Greg, Brittany, and Zack. Although Jim could only stay two nights, Lauryn stayed another week.

The campaign took a new twist in Texas, where Lauryn was asked to speak at a meeting with some prominent scientists. While Jim held another town-hall meeting at a large church, Lauryn met with the scientists in the Space Center's Teague Auditorium.

The first question for Lauryn came from an old friend and classmate from the California Institute of Technology, James Dade. "Lauryn, you and I have known each other for a long time. We asked for this town-hall discussion because there's a strong possibility that you will be the first First Lady of the United States with a doctorate in Astrophysics." There was applause, and Lauryn smiled. "In the position of First Lady, there is much you can do for the overall advancement of science and scientific research."

Lauryn nodded. "Please be more specific, all of you."

A woman in the front row stood up. "I'm Ainsley Schafer, Tours Director here at the Johnson Space Center. Many of the questions we are asked during our tours arise out of what is best described as junk science or pseudo-science. The Internet has nourished its rapid growth, often overshadowing legitimate scientific developments."

"I'm aware of this. There have always been those promoting their personal takes on science that is not supported by legitimate research. It has gotten worse, not just because of the Internet, but also because of the mostly ignorant media not recognizing the difference between pseudo-science and legitimate science. What are you suggesting I can do if I become our country's First Lady?"

Over the nearly three hours that followed, the scientists discussed these challenges. One particular suggestion caught her attention more than the others. Katheryn Suvari, the Director of Livermore National Laboratory, made a comment while talking about another issue, that Lauryn would remember for a long time. "Mrs. Smith, most of us here recognize that there is an overwhelming difference between nuclear fission and nuclear fusion, but no one is interested in pursuing the difference technologically because of the distractions of pseudo-science."

Although Ms. Suvari made the remark about midway through the meeting, it was in the back of Lauryn's mind from then on. What could she do if anything at all?

The campaign continued. Lauryn tried to spend two or three days each month with Brittany and Zack at their home in Sacramento. Jim saw them less frequently. As his ratings went up in the polls, the remarks from traditional politicians became more stridently negative. It was powerfully tempting to respond in kind, but neither Jim nor Lauryn took the bait.

At Adam Paxton's urging, they did not hire a Press Secretary or have others in the campaign speak for them. Every time Jim or Lauryn got on their campaign plane, they talked to the members of the media that were traveling with them. At public appearances, they almost always answered questions, but they avoided responding to questions raised by the other candidates directly. Taking the high road always paid off.

Wherever she went, Lauryn went to luncheons arranged by Adam Paxton, luncheons with women who were leaders in their community. Several times during the campaign, in cities that had foreign embassies, the First Ladies from other countries that knew Lauryn came to the luncheons. Each time, the ratings inched up slightly more.

Lauryn rehearsed Jim for the Presidential debates prior to each one. In the first debate, which was focused upon national security, the Democrat and the Republican focused their attacks on Jim, but Jim was well prepared. The Republican, Ron Evers, was a Senator whom Paul Wilson knew well, After Paul's coaching, Jim could take

Ron Evers apart, politely but effectively. The Democrat, Al Johnson, was Governor of Florida and well understood by Adam Paxton, so Jim was prepared for him as well. All the media said that Jim won the debate.

The second debate was to be about foreign policy. Ron Evers had extensive experience on the Senate Foreign Relations Committee for many years. Senator Evers did not anticipate Lauryn and Jim's vast experience with the leaders of other countries and their thriving network of friends. Jim won that debate even more effectively.

The final debate, on domestic policy, was Jim's almost without preparation, though Adam and Lauryn reviewed his experiences in California thoroughly. Then they were in the home stretch before the election.

In a Labor Day speech, the Republican Ron Evers said, "Jim Smith's wife, Lauryn, couldn't be much of a scientist, simply tagging along for some of his speeches as a Governor." That same day, Democrat Al Johnson said, "Lauryn Smith couldn't be much of a scientist if she was a Christian, and she couldn't be much of a Christian if she was actually a scientist."

In New Orleans, David Cole was still the pastor of a large AME Church. He called Lauryn. "I know we haven't talked since our time together in Houston, but have you heard the idiotic Labor Day comments made by Ron Evers and Al Johnson?"

David could see Lauryn smiling at the other end of their video call. "Oh, I heard them loud and clear. I'm sure God will give me an opportunity to respond."

"Maybe God prompted me to call you!"

"How's that?"

"This coming weekend, my church is hosting its annual Women with Power Conference. We've been advertising it for the last three months. I was going to close the Conference as I usually do, but how would you like to have an opportunity to respond to those two idiots in the same gentle but humorous satirical way in which you and your husband spoke in Houston?"

Lauryn laughed. "David, I'd be happy to! I know where your church is, but what's the day and time I should be there?"

"I think you should come to our Cajun food dinner at 6:00 o'clock next Saturday. Our dinners go long and slow, so I imagine you'll start speaking around 7:30 or so."

"Great! I'll be there! If Jim can be there, he'll come too, okay?"

"We'll be honored." They ended the video call.

Lauryn called Adam Paxton and told him about the call. He let out a whoop. "This is fantastic! It's truly a blessing for you! Jim will be in Boston on Friday, but I will reschedule him for Saturday. Instead of going to New York, I'll have him join you in New Orleans on Saturday. I want you to spend the night in New Orleans, and then you can worship there in David's church on Sunday." This is great!"

Lauryn called David back. "Hey, David, I'm calling you back to let you know that Jim will join me there on Saturday evening, and then we will return to worship with you on Sunday morning."

"Oh... this pleases me immensely, Lauryn. Maybe your husband will consent to get on the piano with our praise team. What do you think?"

"I'll ask him. I think he'll enjoy it. See you on Saturday!"

"Amen!" They ended the call.

Saturday evening, Lauryn began with expressions of thanks. "It's been a long time since Jim and I have enjoyed authentic Cajun food. The food tonight was remarkable. Thank you!" There was applause, stomping of feet, and cheers. "During dinner tonight, your pastor and I had a wonderful discussion of the roles played by Christians among the scientists of our world. He brought it up because of some interesting remarks made by the other two candidates last Monday. Since this is your Annual Women with Power Conference, I'm going to share some things that have happened to me."

Lauryn talked about meeting Jim in church just after getting her bachelor's degree in Astrophysics. She talked about how he has always been supportive of her, including her earning her doctorate. She also talked about Jim working with her with both young children and youth in church as they have raised their four children, including in Sacramento. Then she approached the main point of her speech.

"I had a remarkably interesting experience a few months ago at the Johnson Space Center in Houston. Some scientists asked for a town-hall meeting to talk about possible ways I might be able to help in the advancement of real science if I became first lady. I used the term 'pseudoscience' then and now because there is so much rhetoric masquerading as science on the Internet, the Washington Beltway, and elsewhere. To help you understand where I'm coming from with this, your pastor has arranged to show you a few video clips."

On their large screen, they saw Ron Evers and Al Johnson making their remarks, with booing from the congregation. Then they saw Katheryn Suvari making her comment in Houston.

"The powerful woman you saw in that third clip is Katheryn Suvari, who is the administrative head of the Livermore National Laboratory, a place of advanced atomic research. She and I both have doctorates in physics, though hers is in atomic physics, and my doctorate is in astrophysics. In the months since she said what she did in that video clip, she and I have talked extensively." Lauryn took a sip from a bottle of water.

"Both nuclear fission and nuclear fusion represent huge amounts of energy. We have historically focused upon nuclear fission to make bombs first, and later we have learned to harness nuclear fission to generate electricity. Just north of here, the Waterford Nuclear Generating Station uses nuclear fission to generate your electricity."

There was total silence in the church. "The problem with generating electricity this way is the amount of waste it leaves behind. On the other hand, if we can learn to control nuclear fusion technologically, we can have significantly more electricity, but none of the waste. It will be also much more efficient. So far, governments have not been willing to shoulder the costs or risks associated with developing this technology. Katheryn Suvari and I are talking about ways to enable the private sector to accomplish what the government has not done."

There was murmuring in the congregation. Then Lauryn went on to talk about Sony's giving her the opportunities to explain complex technologies to various audiences around the world. At the end of her speech, she got a standing ovation. While everyone was standing, David offered a closing prayer.

Sunday morning, Jim immensely enjoyed helping the Praise Team lead worship. The church had an eight-foot concert grand piano for Jim to play, while next to him, an excellent artist played an electronic keyboard synthesizer. There were also drums, a string bass, guitars, a trumpet, and a clarinet. The congregation singing God's praise kept wanting more, so the music continued for almost an hour before David began to preach. Then there was another half-hour of music before the benediction.

Unknown to both Lauryn and Jim at the time, both the evening session and the entire worship service were streamed onto the Internet.

5.
Climbing Up

On the election night, they were at the Citizen Hotel in Sacramento, in a suite next to the conference facilities. Most of their campaign team was there or nearby. In the ballroom was a live band with hundreds of people. When Jim was declared the winner with 73% of the vote, Lauryn kissed him passionately. Then she said, "We jumped off this cliff together. Now we have to start climbing up!"

"The first time I need to climb is this chair and table." As everyone on the team began cheering, he smiled and gestured for quiet. "Thank you, everyone, for all of your hard work. Adam, this has been an amazing roller-coaster ride!" Adam bowed and saluted. "Now I have to head to the ballroom and make a little speech, so the rest of you can relax, celebrate, or do what you planned to do when we win, because we've won!" There was cheering as he climbed down.

Lauren took his arm as they went down the hall to the ballroom, where the band had stopped playing because of the cheering. They went to the mike, and Jim offered a spontaneous rambling speech that everyone applauded and cheered, but he hated later. The audience cheered even more when Tony, Abby, Claudia, Greg, Brittany, and Zack joined Lauryn and Jim on the stage, and they were smiling and waving.

The Secret Service had a motorcade waiting to take them back to their house in River Park. The police had their neighborhood sealed off except for the residents. The next morning, they slept in. As planned, their breakfast on Wednesday morning was catered. Although Lauryn and Jim would fly to Washington the following Monday for a week, there was a lot to do in Sacramento before then.

Their Sacramento house would go up for sale soon enough, but in the meantime, Jim would begin interviewing people for both staff and cabinet positions, using the spacious office there in the house. Many of the people he got to know during the campaign would stay on to be with his administration in various capacities.

Before Jim could do that, however, he and Lauryn went and sat down outside in their back yard. There were plenty of trees to give them privacy, and the Secret Service stayed out of sight most of the time. Sitting beside a patio table, they both had tall glasses of iced tea, with a large pitcher filled with refills.

Lauryn spoke softly. "Jim, I think I decided what I wanted to do as First Lady before we went to New Orleans and to Dave's church." She sipped some tea. "Even though I love being at your side, I expect that most of the time we'll see each other in our residence at the White House. I know that you won't be able to share most of your work with me."

Jim nodded. "Yes. I'll choose a Chief of Staff by the end of this month, and I think you should too."

"That's going to be hard, Jim. I want someone who knows how to make things happen in Washington, but she should also have significant science chops. I'm not sure that Paul Wilson can help, but he might. Come to think of it, many of the people I talked with at the Johnson Space Center are either ex-military or familiar with Washington Beltway politics. You and I are going to be making many phone calls!"

"We're simply going to have to keep our work separate, Lauryn."

"I agree."

Those days between the election and January 20th were a blur of activity. Among all the other things they did together, however, was her helping Jim write his first inaugural address.

On Inauguration Day itself, much of what happened was similar to a military operation. Officers from the General Services Administration were moving the Stallings administration's people out while moving the Smith administration in, including doing some painting and changing some of the carpeting. It was a rapid 12 hours that got it done for Lauryn and Jim. The General Services crew was there until after midnight to complete their job. All the personal decor choices that needed to be changed had to take place after January 20th.

While Jim was beginning his work as President, Lauryn was in their residence helping Brittany and Zack get settled. They had already selected a public high school to attend. They would not see Tony, Abby, Claudia, and Greg until they went to Camp David to celebrate Memorial Day.

A surprise began with a phone call that first afternoon in the White House residence. "Mrs. Smith, this is the White House operator. I have a call for you from a Mr. James Dade."

"Yes! Put him through. Hi, Jim!"

"Congratulations, Lauryn. I imagine you're getting ready for this evening's inaugural ball, but I wanted to call you before you get too busy."

"I'm glad you called. I enjoyed seeing you and Leslie again in Houston at the town-hall meeting."

"We enjoyed seeing you too. Leslie reminded me a few minutes ago that you're probably searching for a Chief of Staff for yourself unless you've already chosen one."

Lauryn sat down. "No, I've not chosen one yet. It needs to be a woman who knows how to make things happen here in the Washington Beltway, and who also has a strong science background. I know it is a tall order."

Jim Dade now spoke more confidently. "When I was working full-time for NASA, Leslie and I got to know many people there inside the Beltway. We know exactly who you need. Her name is Veronica Miller. Most people call her Ronnie. She's about your age, and she has always been totally non-partisan because for most of twenty years, she worked for special-interest groups. She is also a lay leader at The Church of the Advent, which is an Anglican church there in D.C. She's as honest as anyone I've ever met, and she's a mover and shaker when she needs to be. Ronnie is the widow of a professor who taught Physics at M.I.T. She also has a Ph.D. in physics, but while her husband was alive, she enjoyed being a doting housewife."

Lauryn felt like a huge weight had been lifted from her shoulders. "Jim, she sounds perfect."

"Leslie is sending you an email right now with all of her particulars. We probably won't be talking again, except rarely, so Leslie and I wish you and Jim the best. We'll be praying for the two of you to last a full eight years."

"Thank you, Jim. Thank Leslie for me! Bye!" The call ended. Lauryn checked her email. After saving the information to her contacts, she called the White House operator. "Hi. I'm going to be expecting a call from Veronica Miller. Will you please put her on my contacts list?"

"Yes, Mrs. Smith."

"Thank you." Lauryn hung up and sent a text to Veronica Miller to phone her at the White House. Less than a minute passed before her desk phone rang. "Hello?"

"Mrs. Smith, this is Veronica Miller."

"Yes! I was talking to an old friend of mine, Jim Dade. He has recommended you to me to be my Chief of Staff. If you're interested, how soon can you be here?"

"I'm definitely interested. I can be there in about fifteen minutes."

"Excellent! I'll see you in fifteen." Lauryn hung up, and then she called Security. "This is Lauryn Smith. I'm expecting a woman named Veronica Miller to arrive in about fifteen minutes. I'd like her cleared, and I am sending the Chief Usher, for her."

"Very good. We'll take care of it."

"Thank you, very much, I appreciate it." She disconnected and dialed a number on the laminated directory in front of her.

"Chief Usher's Office, David Garner speaking."

"David, this is Lauryn Smith. I think my new Chief of Staff is going to be Veronica Miller. She will be arriving in less than fifteen minutes. Will you please have her brought to my office when she's cleared security?"

"Yes, of course. I will take care of Mrs. Miller."

"Thank you, David." The call ended.

Jim Dade had been right. About ten minutes later, the Chief Usher arrived with Lauryn's future Chief of Staff, and she looked remarkably like one of her classmates at C.I.T. "Veronica!" They shook hands. "It is good to meet you. You remind me of a woman who was in my doctoral colloquium many years ago."

"Really! Call me Ronnie. Are you talking about someone at C.I.T.? That's where you got your sheepskin in Astrophysics, right?"

"Yes. You did yours at M.I.T., didn't you? Let's sit down." They sat down in a conversation area that was left over by the previous First Lady. "Ronnie, you fit the special qualifications that I need in a Chief of Staff, so I put the word out to Jim Dade and his friends in Houston."

"Really! How may I serve you here?"

"As I told my husband late on election day, I want someone who knows how to make things happen in

Washington, but she should also have significant science chops. That's you, Ronnie."

"You need my science background? I've seldom had occasion even to refer to my physics background as I've worked here in Washington. This sounds like fun!"

Lauryn grinned. "I hope it'll be some fun, but it will also be hard work. In my years of representing Sony in various countries, I've developed contacts and friends, including many women who are the wives of political leaders. I'll show you my complete contacts list when you begin to get settled. Which brings us to the point, will you be my Chief of Staff?"

Ronnie's mouth hung open for a moment. "I'd be honored, Mrs. Smith!"

"I'm Lauryn if you're Ronnie. As soon as my husband picks an Ambassador to the U.N., the Ambassador, you, and I are going to set up a 'tea,' for which we will invite the spouses of all the ambassadors. I want to build a network there. If our ambassador is a woman, she'll hopefully be part of our network."

"Fascinating!"

"When I give you a copy of my contacts list, you'll need to commit as much of it as you can to memory. For instance, the current ambassador from India to the U.N. undoubtedly knows the First Lady of India. I do too. That network will involve one part of my work as First Lady."

"That's just one part?"

"Correct. Almost a year ago, when Jim and I were on the campaign trail, I was invited to a town-hall meeting at the Johnson Space Center. It was hosted by Ainsley Schafer. You probably know her."

"Yes, Ainsley and I have known each other for years."

"Good. Call her and ask her to send you a video copy of that meeting. That will give you a good picture of the second part of my work as First Lady. This brings us to the third and final major part of the work I want to do. From time to time, my husband and I will come up with something in the first two areas that will require congressional support."

Ronnie nodded. "I'll be finding senators and/or congressmen to come up with a bill, and you'll need me to work with the rest of the White House staff to get the legislation passed."

Lauryn smiled. "We're understanding each other already, Ronnie." She picked up the desk handset and dialed. "David, I need to have you show Ronnie her office. It might also be a good time for you to orient her and introduce her to some of your staff as well."

"Yes, I'll be right there."

Lauryn looked at Ronnie. "We're off and running." David Garner arrived, and he and Ronnie left for her new office.

Dinner that evening was after 8:00. Jim gave Lauryn a hug and a kiss. "Wow am I hungry! Are you?"

Lauryn nodded. "Famished! I hired my Chief of Staff this afternoon, a woman named Veronica Miller. She wants to be called Ronnie. Do you think you'll be able to get Amber Heigl approved as U.N. Ambassador?"

He held her chair for her. "I don't think it'll be a problem. Assuming there's no holdup in the Senate, she'll probably be installed at the end of next week." He sat down, and they were served their soup.

"Ronnie and I will want to have a meeting with Amber as soon as she is confirmed."

"Right. I've told her about your wanting to establish a women's support network."

They only had about a half-hour for dinner before Jim had to return to the Oval Office. Lauryn went back to her office and printed out her contacts list for Ronnie. There was a knock on her office door, and Phil Kaiser stood in the doorway. "May I come in?"

"Of course, Phil, what's up?"

"I just need to remind you to use only your personal cell phone for calls to family members and close friends, where your official business as First Lady is not involved. Otherwise, please either go through the White House Operator or use the secure cell phone that we of the Secret Service have provided to you."

Lauryn nodded. "I remember you saying something similar when we first got acquainted with you at the Sacramento Airport."

He nodded. "Yes. I understand Veronica Miller is going to be your Chief of Staff."

"Yes. I like her."

"I will brief her on Secret Service policies and procedures tomorrow morning."

"I think you'll like her, Phil. She's a non-partisan just like Jim and me."

He nodded. "If there's nothing else, I'll be going."

"Okay. Good night, Phil." He left, and Lauryn headed back to the residence. As she stepped into their bedroom, she stood in the middle of the room and looked all around. Then she took out her secure cell phone and sent a text to the decorator from the General Services Administration that had done so much.

> Thank you for doing such a beautiful job redecorating our private quarters as well as public areas. You do beautiful work.

Lauryn was reading in bed when Jim came back in from the Oval Office. "Good evening, my love."

He leaned in and kissed her. "Good evening. I think I need a shower before going to bed. Would you like to join me?"

"Sure! You don't have to ask twice!"

It was just shy of midnight when they finally turned off the light. The super insulated room was wonderfully quiet. They were both asleep immediately.

As Lauryn's Chief of Staff signed in at the Security desk the next morning, the Secret Service was waiting. "Mrs. Miller, I'm Phil Kaiser with the Secret Service."

"Everyone calls me Ronnie. You can too."

They started walking. "Very well, Ronnie. Before you begin to get busy this morning, I'm going to brief you on Secret Service policies and procedures. You've already met Bob Hackman at your apartment this morning. He is in command of your personal detail." For the next half hour, Ronnie learned all she needed to know regarding how secure her safety was going to be because she works at the White House.

When Ronnie walked into Lauryn's office, she was already there at her computer terminal. "Good morning, Lauryn. I've just got my briefing from Phil Kaiser."

"Good! He told me last evening that he was going to brief you the first thing this morning. It looks like we'll get Amber Heigl approved as U.N. Ambassador by the Senate, unless there are any snags."

"Right. My sources say that Senator Alex Jefferson was trying to get someone else considered but had to give up. It seems your husband either has friends on both sides of the aisle, or there are senators who will want favors returned at a later time. Both are probably true."

"Good. I want you and me to meet with Amber as soon as she is confirmed."

"I'll set it up. I have previously dealt with her in my lobbying days."

"You're going to have a visit from someone from the GSA sometime this morning. They'll decorate your office more to your tastes, but you have to indicate what you want. That little suite is going to be your home away from home. At the top of our priorities during the next week or so is for you to hire more staff for us. They all have to understand three essential things. If they do their job, don't screw up legally, and never lie to anyone here, you and I will stand by them through everything else. Never lying might be hard for some of them. Just know that I have decided to trust you."

"I know. I trust you too. You and I think so much alike. It's uncanny."

"That's one of the reasons I hired you. By the way, I want you to join my husband and me this evening for dinner. Will that be a problem?"

"No, I'm looking forward to meeting The President."

"His Chief of Staff will be joining us as well."

Ronnie smiled. "Excellent! I've not seen or talked with Jay Fillion in several years. In addition to his neutral political gifts, he's a handsome dude."

Lauryn smiled. "Did you know his wife died last August? She died of ovarian cancer less than a month after she was diagnosed. It was sad."

"Oh. I hadn't heard. Thanks for telling me. I'll be careful this evening." She paused, thoughtful. "Paul and Dot Wilson are friends of yours, aren't they?"

"Yes. I haven't seen Dot since we saw her in Houston almost a year ago. Why do you ask?"

"Well, of all the women I've ever met, Dot knows how to work a crowd better than anyone. If she walks into a room full of fifty women, she can have most of them thinking about what she's thinking in less than an hour. I suggest that you ask Dot to help us with our networking."

Lauryn was thoughtful. "I hadn't thought of her in that way. That's a great idea!

The dinner that night was enjoyable for all of them. Jim and Jay could be with them for more than an hour before they had to return to the Oval Office.

6.
Networking

Lauryn was putting on makeup, and Jim was shaving early one Sunday morning, when Lauryn's personal cell phone rang. Their youngest daughter's face appeared on the screen. Lauryn touched the speaker button. "Good morning Brittany! This sure is early for you!"

Jim leaned over to get into the camera's range. "Hi Brittany!"

"Hi Dad! Hi Mom! I had to set an alarm. The sun won't rise out here for another hour. I wanted to call before either of you got busy."

Lauryn smiled. "What's up, girl?"

"It's two things. First, Zack told me to tell you that he'll be there for a short visit this evening."

"Really! You're not coming?" Jim turned off his razor.

"Not this time, Dad. Zack's been rehearsing with the praise team for Pastor Li Jie. Zack will be on drums when they put on an evangelism event next week in New Delhi."

Lauryn was as surprised as Jim. "You're going to be in New Delhi with Li Jie? [Pronounced *lee gee-ah*] That Chinese evangelist has really made a name for himself in the last few years. So, Zack will be here this evening?"

"Right. He expects to be there in time for dinner." Jim's secure cell rang. "Excuse me, Brittany, but I have to take this call." He was done shaving, so he went back into the bedroom while Lauryn continued with Brittany.

"How are things going with your boyfriend, Mason?"

"Oh, Mom, he's asked me to marry him, and I said yes!"

"Whoa! That's great, Brittany."

"We're not going to move in together, because I'm firm with him on that. Tonight, Tony and Abby will be here, along with Claudia and Greg, and Mason and I will tell them during dinner. So far, I have no idea when the wedding will be."

"Is Mason still majoring in Forestry there at Sierra College?"

"Yeah, and he'll finish his bachelor's in Forestry this May. The National Park Service wants to put him to work in Redwoods National Park. That's more than six hours away, so if he goes there it will put some strain on our relationship."

"Just between us, have you thought about having a White House wedding?"

Brittany turned red, as Lauryn could see on the phone. "Mason and I talked about that possibility last night, but we agree that it just isn't us."

Lauryn was thoughtful. "I'm thinking of a compromise that would please your Dad and me."

"A compromise?"

"Yeah. You could have a relatively small ceremony in Shenandoah National Park, and then we could put on a reception here in the White House."

"I'll have to talk to Mason about it, but that might work for us."

Lauryn nodded. "Your Dad will not be willing to pull strings for you and Mason, but your Mom would love it if, as a married couple, Mason got called to serve in that park."

"I know Dad wouldn't pull strings, and I'm not sure that Mason would like to serve in that park. He can I can discuss it, though."

"Girl, if Mason really wants to serve in Shenandoah National Park and applies there, my Chief of Staff could see to it that the park service notices his application."

"Mom! You're not into conspiracies!"

"Well, I'm your Mom."

That evening, Zack visited with both his parents for about an hour over dinner, and after The President returned to the Oval Office, he talked with Lauryn until after midnight, when his Dad returned from the Oval Office, and they talked for another half-hour before Zack went to a guest room to sleep. He had an early flight the next morning.

The next day being Sunday, Lauryn and Jim would have liked to go to a church in the Beltway for worship, but that call on Jim's phone had taken him to the Situation Room in the basement. Lauryn wouldn't see him for the rest of the day and much of the evening. She attended a worship service for staff there in the White House.

When Lauryn went into her office on Monday morning, Ronnie was already there. "Good morning, Ronnie."

"Good morning, Lauryn. I understand your youngest son was here over the weekend."

"Yes, it was an enjoyable but short visit. He had to leave early Sunday morning for New Delhi, where he will be a praise team drummer for the evangelist, Li Jie."

"New Delhi! You and the President have some powerful friends there."

"Yes. We talked about them with Zack over dinner Saturday evening." We learned Zack was coming early Saturday morning from our youngest daughter, Brittany. She became engaged to her boyfriend on Friday night." Lauryn then told Ronnie about that conversation in detail.

"You were right. If Mason applies, and when the mail is opened, I can make sure someone way low in the ranks makes the connection between Mason and your daughter. It only takes one phone call to an anonymous friend."

Lauryn nodded. "We'll have to wait and see if Mason applies."

"Right. Most of the day today I'm interviewing possible staff members in the lounge downstairs. If you need me, I'll be there."

"Okay, but I'm going to be taking a helicopter to New York this morning and going over to the U.N. to reconnect with two or three old friends there. I'm hoping that when the media sees me leaving, that they won't go into too much of a frenzy. Then, if Amber can meet with us towards the end of next week, I'll be able to tell her about some network friends that are already established at the U.N."

"Can I tell staff applicants that you're in New York today?" Lauryn responded with a puzzled look. Ronnie went on. "It'll be a good test to see how well they can control their tongues."

Lauryn nodded. "That's probably a good idea, Ronnie. Did you locate the three women at the U.N. that we identified?"

She handed the First Lady a slip of paper. "I gave the information to the Secret Service yesterday afternoon. Your escorts will take you to all three women. All you have to do is stay with your escorts. I wish I could go with you, but without other staff available yet, I need to remain back here."

Lauryn nodded. "I'll be fine. This first casual trip needs to happen today. You go ahead with your work."

"Okay." Ronnie walked out.

Lauryn looked at her watch. It was time for her to get to the Limo that would take her to Andrews Air Force Base. The first leg of her trip to the U.N. didn't take long.

She had never flown in a helicopter, let alone a big military one like the luxury-modified Eurocopter UH-72 Lakota. It was comfortable and much quieter than she expected. As they took off, she got Phil Kaiser's attention. "I want to see Juliette Debré first if possible."

He nodded. "Madame Debré knows you're coming. We'll arrive at the diplomats' entrance, and she should be just inside. You'll be meeting the other two in one of the conference rooms. Just stay with me."

The flight took less than an hour, and the limo ride to the diplomats' entrance of the United Nations Building complex was also brief. Just after entering, Lauryn approached the wife of the former Prime Minister of France, now the Ambassador. "Madam Debré! Juliette! Bonjour!"

Juliette spoke flawless English. "Good morning, Lauryn! It is good to see you again!" They hugged. "I've been looking forward to this. My involvement with my husband's work as Ambassador of France is often so boring, formal, and routine. This should be an interesting day."

Phil Kaiser led the way as they began walking. Lauryn spoke more softly as they walked along. "You and I are meeting two others in one of the smaller conference rooms where we'll reconnect with one another. I think you know both of them."

Juliette smiled. "Oh yes, though we don't get to talk as much as you might think."

"I'm hoping to change that." They went into the conference room, and a porter approached them. "Good morning."

"Good morning, First Lady Smith. I am Shultz. I will be available to you for as much as you need me. There are beverages and snacks on hand for all four of you. All you have to do is ask."

Lauryn smiled and nodded. "Good. We will probably be eating lunch at about noon."

Schultz gave a slight bow. "Very good!" He turned and walked away.

Lauryn sat down at a round table. "Juliette, I remember vividly when we first met in Paris. Your husband expressed interest in the Sony products I was introducing, but he was even more interested in talking to my husband and me about American politics. When the four of us had lunch together, I was startled by our mutual love of broiled grapefruit as a dessert."

Juliette laughed. "I think you and I bonded as friends because of that!" She looked towards the door. "Here are the others, and one more."

Lauryn first greeted Maria Cedronio, wife of the Ambassador from Italy. "Maria! It has been too long!"

"Yes!" They hugged. "Lauryn, have you met Jillian Wright? She's the wife of Sir John Cromer, the Ambassador from the United Kingdom."

Lauryn smiled and offered her hand. "It is wonderful to meet you at last, Jillian. I have heard so much about you from our mutual friend, Ainsley Schafer, who works at our Johnson Space Center."

Jillian smiled. "Yes, Ainsley and I were roommates in Hollis Hall at Harvard." She turned. "I didn't think you'd mind if I brought along a friend of mine. This is Margret Thors. Her husband, Hans Thors, is the Icelandic Ambassador."

Margret's smile was broad and infectious as she reached out her hand. "First Lady Smith, it is a genuine pleasure to meet you!"

"You can call me Lauryn if I can call you Margret. It is a pleasure to meet you as well. Let's all sit down."

Lauryn asked Shultz for a cup of Earl Grey tea, and the others did as well. After sipping some of her tea, Lauryn began. "I wanted to have this meeting out of a desire to have a strong network. It all began years ago in Paris, which is why I'm particularly glad that Juliette is here. In my many years of representing Sony in countries around the world, I've developed quite a number of contacts and friends, including many women who are the wives of political leaders like yourselves."

During the next five hours, old friendships were refreshed, and new friendships were established. In the late afternoon, when she got into the Limo, she was upbeat but tired. "Phil, this has been a full but rewarding day. In future meetings like this one, I plan on having a couple of staff members with me to help carry the conversational load – particularly Ronnie."

He nodded. "I understand."

Just over an hour later, Ronnie was still there when Lauryn walked into her office. "Hey Ronnie."

"Hi! How did the day go?"

"It was both exhausting and rewarding. For future meetings, I want you to come along to help carry the conversational load. You'll enjoy meeting Juliette Debré. She is a real treasure. Maria Cedronio is also a woman whose friendship I enjoy. As expected, Jillian Wright was there. She's brilliant, and she shares our friendship with Ainsley Schafer. Unexpectedly, Jillian brought along another diplomat's wife. Her name is Margret Thors. Her husband, Hans Thors, is the Icelandic Ambassador. I'm glad she joined us. Margret has a smile that lights up a room. I recorded the entire meeting on my secured cell phone. I want someone on our staff to transcribe it."

Ronnie nodded. "Speaking of staff, I've hired two men and a woman. There's another that wants to pray about it with her husband."

"She wants to pray with her husband. That's my kind of people."

"Yes." Ronnie went to the door to the outer office area and gestured the new staff in. "This is our staff so far, Ma'am. "First, this is Jason Pounds."

"Hi Jason." She shook his hand.

"Among his other abilities, he gets computers to do their things better than they're originally programmed to do. He can also get computers to do new things by creating new programs."

Ronnie turned to a girl who looked like she was Brittany's age. "This is Marnette Phipps. She does many things well. As a bonus, she has two black belts."

"It's nice to meet you Marnette."

"It's great to meet you, Ma'am. Last year, I read your paper on the radiation variations from Alpha Centauri, and I was fascinated."

Lauryn was startled. "I've not thought about that project for years! I wrote it when I was in my early twenties."

Marnette smiled. "Yes, Ma'am. That paper inspired me to register with the University of Phoenix. I've started work on my master's degree in nuclear chemistry."

Lauryn raised her eyebrows and nodded.

Ronnie pointed at another man. "Finally, this third guy is Gary Scorupco. He has been working on Paul Wilson's staff for five years. He told Senator Wilson that he wanted to get away from working in the legislative branch, and Paul called me."

Lauryn shook his hand. "Paul and Dot Wilson are good friends of mine. Since Paul has suggested that you work with me, I trust his judgment. Besides, if you let me down, I'll never let Dot hear the last of it!"

He smiled. "I'll do my best."

"Ronnie, which one of these three do you think would be best at transcribing my meeting today?"

"I think Jason is probably your best bet. We can utilize his computer skills another day."

"Jason, are you any good at transcribing?"

"I can do about a hundred fifty words a minute with common vocabulary."

"Okay." She handed him her phone. "Download my audio file I recorded today, and then get started the first thing tomorrow morning on it. It could be a long job. There are five women's voices on there. Ronnie will give you their names. Download it right now, and then give me the phone back. I have two, but that's my secured phone."

"Yes, Ma'am."

"Ronnie, after we meet with Veronica, get started on setting up our next networking meeting. Jason, we'll need to set up a secured network file. Gary, I need suggestions from you to establish a list of non-partisan people we can trust here in the Washington Beltway. Marnette, has Ronnie given any assignments to you yet?"

"No ma'am. She hired me less than fifteen minutes before you returned from New York."

Lauryn nodded. "Okay. Right now, I want you to explore the West Wing casually. Start to get to know the support staff. Find some people you'd like to have lunch with there from time to time. It's not a matter of spying. It's just that Ronnie and I will be having to work with the West Wing, and it's good to know who we can talk with there when the major players are not available."

Ronnie nodded. "Remember to share with them only the things we want people to know about. You'll be like a gatekeeper for us."

"Okay."

That evening, Jim could get away to the residence for an early dinner. He greeted her with a hug and kiss. "Do you see any gray hairs with me yet?" He grinned.

Lauryn looked at him carefully. "Not yet. I met with four women for five hours at the U.N. today."

They sat down at the table in their dining room. "Would I have liked to be a fly on the wall at that meeting?"

"Maybe. Someone on my staff will transcribe the meeting tomorrow. Things that most men would consider small talk might turn out to be important to us later."

After their salads were put in front of them, Lauryn offered a prayer, and then they began to eat. "Jim, an unexpected attendee to the meeting was the wife of the

Icelandic Ambassador. Her name is Margret Thors. I like her."

Jim nodded as he ate. "In all of our travels together, we've never gotten back to Iceland since our honeymoon, like we planned."

"I know. We even talked about taking our kids there."

They had a leisurely dinner, but then Jim returned to the Oval Office.

7.
Fusion Talk

Three weeks later, early on Monday morning, Amber Heigl met with Lauryn and her staff. The new U.S. Ambassador to the United Nations was fascinated. "This network sounds like it is developing into something that can be very useful."

Lauryn nodded. "We hope so. Please understand, Amber, that I'm not suggesting that you be part of the network – at least not while you're our country's ambassador. I don't think that would be appropriate, and the media would create all kinds of conspiracy theories."

Amber laughed. "You're probably right."

"Having said that, I'm thinking that the network might be useful to you from time to time. Spouses in the inside of political operations sometimes know practical information that our intelligence services don't know."

The ambassador nodded. "I don't doubt that. You and I can maintain a casual friendship without overtly involving the network."

Lauryn nodded. "I agree, Amber."

The meeting lasted less than a half hour, but a friendship was begun. Lauryn was satisfied as Amber left. "Ronnie, I need time to think and pray. I'll be here in my office, if necessary."

"Yes Ma'am." Ronnie and the staff walked out.

Lauryn went to the large window and stared out at the cityscape. She prayed softly. "Lord God, my mind keeps going back to the Johnson Space Center meeting and what

Katheryn Suvari said to me there. I surrendered that conversation to you a long time ago, but have you been preparing either of us to go forward?" Lauryn continued to stare at the cityscape as she let herself become aware of God's continuing presence. Hundreds of images flashed through her mind at lightning speed. "Thank you, Lord. Amen."

She sat down at her desk, picked up the desk handset, and dialed the operator. "This is Lauryn Smith. I need to talk to Katheryn Suvari at the Lawrence Livermore National Laboratory."

"Yes. When we reach her, I'll put her through to you."

"Thank you." Lauryn hung up and leaned back in her chair. She was deep in thought when the phone rang. She picked up the handset.

"I have Katheryn Suvari for you."

"Thank you. "Kathy! We haven't talked since our meeting in Houston! I wish we could talk privately and in person!"

"Yes! You're the First Lady now, so what are you thinking with regard to the huge challenge we discussed?" They both knew that their conversation might be recorded.

"Kathy, getting federal funding to pursue it could take forever, if at all. We need to find ways to stimulate the private sector. Is there any way you could come to Washington for a few days, so that we can discuss this more thoroughly? My Chief of Staff also has her Ph.D. in Physics, so she wants to meet you too."

"This sounds great! How about next weekend? If I fly to Washington on Friday, I can stay until Monday."

"Okay, Kathy, I'll have Ronnie make a reservation for you at eDreams, okay?"

"Okay, Lauryn, see you on Friday."

She hung up and pushed a button. "Ronnie, make a reservation for Katheryn Suvari to stay at eDreams next weekend, from Friday to Monday. I hope this won't ruin your weekend."

"No Lauryn. I'm already looking forward to this."

"Good. You understand our challenges."

"Absolutely. I'll meet her at the airport on Friday."

That week's days flew by rapidly. Lauryn's staff settled into their routines and challenges. After prayer, another staff member became part of the team. Her name was Jill Turk.

Friday afternoon, Ronnie kept track of when Katheryn Suvari's flight would arrive, and she left the office in time to meet her. She had a printed sign saying, 'Suvari,' and Katheryn approached her. "You must be Ronnie!" She held out her hand.

"Yes, and you're Kathy. I recognize you from your federal file." They shook hands. "I'll take you to eDreams, where you can freshen up. The hotel is only a few blocks from the White House. You and I will be having dinner with the President and First Lady at 7:00." They got into a taxi. "Take us to eDreams, please." She turned back to Kathy. "If you want to walk to the White House, I can meet you at the security desk at 6:45, or I can pick you up at the hotel at about 6:30 or so."

Kathy nodded. "I think I'd like to walk. It's a beautiful day, and after sitting in a plane for so many hours, the exercise will be good."

"Okay. Your expenses will be covered at eDreams. Here we are." The taxi stopped in front of the hotel. "I'll see you at 6:45."

"Right." Kathy got out and closed the door."

"Now to the White House." The taxi rolled ahead.

When Kathy and Ronnie walked into the residence dining room, Lauryn and Jim were already there. Jim greeted her. "Hello! I'm President Smith. Lauryn has told me quite a bit about you." They shook hands.

"I've been looking forward to meeting you, President Smith." She meant it.

"Here in the residence, you can call me Jim. Let's sit down."

As they ate their salads, they made small talk. When the soup had been put in front of them, Jim said, I want to hear you talk, Kathy. Why don't you begin by giving me your description of the difference between nuclear fission and nuclear fusion?"

Kathy took a spoonful of soup, and then she put her spoon down. "Fusion energy is the opposite of energy from fission, which comes from splitting an atom. Fission is widely used to power nuclear plants and weapons. Conversely, fusion occurs constantly on the surface of our sun, where most of the sun's energy comes by way of the nuclear fusion of hydrogen and helium. That makes a heavier nucleus and produces a little leftover energy during the process. When those nuclei fuse, they create more energy."

The President nodded. "I take it that, as simple as that sounds, the big challenge involves the heat. Ronnie, you, and Lauryn have been talking about this for quite a while. What about the heat?"

"Here on Earth, the amount of energy you would need to put in, to produce that kind of heat or pressure to start fusion is much higher than what you get out in usable energy. On the other hand, fusion does not produce runaway chain reactions, so there is no possibility of a meltdown. Fusion reactions do not produce much radioactive waste either. For fusion to occur on Earth, apart from the sun, we need a temperature of 180 million degrees Fahrenheit—six times hotter than the sun's core."

Jim stopped eating. "Say again?"

Ronnie smiled. "180 million degrees."

He smiled. "Lauryn, I remember back when we were first married there was a media buzz about cold fusion. Didn't that work out?"

She grinned and shook her head. "Cold fusion is a myth. Scientists are still working on making hot fusion a viable energy source, but it is a huge scientific challenge. Fusion reactions do occur inside tokamaks, which are doughnut-shaped chambers where gas is pumped into a vacuum chamber and electricity flows through the center. The gas becomes charged, forming plasma that is locked inside the vacuum chamber by magnetic fields, which is similar to the pressure at the sun's core. Radio and microwaves are fired into the plasma to raise its temperature, and at around 180 million degrees fusion occurs. The primary barrier to a sustained reaction, other than the high cost of the electricity needed to heat the chamber, is finding a material that can withstand that much heat for more than a few seconds."

Again, he nodded. "That seems impossible, but we all know that getting federal funding for such a difficult and dangerous project is close to impossible."

They were finished with their soup, and the dishes were taken away as broiled halibut was put in front of them.

When the waiters had left, Kathy responded to what the President had said. "Mr. President – Jim - the main barrier to generating energy through a fusion reaction is typically defined in terms of getting government funding, as you said. Every time there's talk about climate change, funding for it rises for a while, but there has never been enough funding to get the first power plants built. For less than $50 billion, we could build a working reactor, but it would probably not be dependable. Our question becomes now whether we can make it both reliable and affordable."

Lauryn picked up on that thought. "Kathy and I are thinking in terms of approaching this the way they did at Los Alamos in 1942 to produce the first bomb. We can break up the project into smaller challenges to be taken on by the private sector. Some of these smaller issues are of interest to the military. The Department of Defense has a way of finding a few billion to fund their own interests when they want to."

Ronnie nodded. "Lauryn spoke of finding material to endure the heat. Another possible approach would be to develop technology to divert the heat for another purpose."

Kathy stared at her. "Ronnie! I'd never thought of that. It's brilliant! Some of our current nuclear trigger technology might be able to be redeveloped for that purpose."

On that particular Friday evening, there were no emergencies, so the President did not have to return to the Oval Office. The dinner hour turned into two. When the women went back to Lauryn's office for more planning, Jim spent time catching up on his reading. Kathy returned to her hotel at shortly after midnight.

Saturday morning, before Ronnie and Kathy got to her office, Lauryn picked up the handset at her desk. "Operator, I need to speak with the Director of the F.B.I."

"Just a moment."

"F.B.I., Edgar Wesson."

"Mr. Wesson, this is the First Lady, Lauryn Smith. I'm glad you are there this morning."

"Yes, Ma'am, what can I do for you?

"Last evening, Katheryn Suvari, the Director of Livermore National Laboratory, and my Chief of Staff, Veronica Miller, joined the President and I for dinner. I have some security concerns."

"Security concerns? How so?"

"I assume my husband has 'Top Secret' security clearance, as does Katheryn Suvari, but to the best of my knowledge, neither I nor my Chief of Staff have such security clearance. All three of us women have doctorates in physics, and last night our discussions got highly technical.

I don't want to take any chances that one of us could inadvertently violate the law. I would like to get security clearances for both myself and my Chief of Staff."

"Did the President ask you to call me?"

"No. Last night, we discussed these concerns, but he left it to me to handle our concerns as I see fit. He and I have been a team since we got married."

"Evidently, I failed to make some things sufficiently clear to your husband. The security clearance system itself is an expression of presidential authority. Its scope and operation are defined in an executive order, and its terms can be modified by your husband. I think I told him this during his first few days in office, but he was given a lot of information in a short time, so this may have slipped his mind. If your husband wishes to grant access to classified information to a family member, for example, there would be no legal barrier to doing so. To make this official, I'll call him and remind him right now. Then everything is up to him."

"Thank you, Mr. Wesson. I'm sorry to have bothered you on a Saturday."

"It's no bother, Ma'am. It's part of my job. Have a good weekend."

"Thank you, again."

"You're welcome." They hung up.

There was a soft knock, and Ronnie came in with Kathy. "Good morning! You're here early, Lauryn."

Lauryn nodded. "Yes. My husband and I continued talking about fusion last night for another hour or so after you two left. The only thing I've done so far this morning is put in a call to Edgar Wesson." Her desk phone rang, and she picked up the handset.

"It's me. I just had a call from Edgar Wesson. He reminded me of my powers regarding security. I had forgotten it amid the shuffle of the first few days."

She smiled. "He told me he was going to call you."

"Right. I told him I was granting you and Ronnie full clearance on everything. I simply remind you that if any of you release classified information without proper clearance, it will be a federal felony. Okay?"

"Okay. Thank you, my love. See you tonight."

"Right. I love you too." He hung up.

Lauryn looked at Ronnie and Kathy. "Okay, ladies, as of this moment, all three of us have security clearance as high as it goes. If we spill classified information outside of our group, it will be a federal felony."

Kathy bursts out laughing. "I like his style!"

Ronnie was smiling. "This is a first I never thought I'd have. Security clearance! Wow!"

Lauryn nodded. "Kathy, I thought of something when I woke up this morning. Reflecting on the idea of surrounding the fusion with technology other than a solid insulative material, what about the Leidenfrost effect? At hotter than a liquid's boiling point, the effect produces an insulating vapor layer. This was discussed years ago on an episode of *Mythbusters*, broadcast by PBS. If, for instance, tungsten powder is injected into the plasma, and the fusion reaction is surrounded with liquid tungsten...."

Kathy's eyes got big. "The effect would still insulate, and the powder would adhere to the liquid as the effect continued!"

Ronnie stared at the two of them. "It just **might** work!" She paused. "The military might be able to apply the same Leidenfrost effect to the laser cannons that are still being developed. The military might help fund the research of the Leidenfrost effect without our even mentioning its possible application to fusion."

Their brainstorming continued the rest of the day. That evening, the topic around the dinner table was Dr. Johann Gottlob Leidenfrost and the effect he first described. Jim was fascinated. The women lost him, however, when they described how it might be applied by the military or by fusion.

Sunday morning, the Secret Service suggested that they could worship at Church of the Advent, which is an Anglican Church that Lauryn and Jim liked. Afterward, they all agreed that they had truly worshiped. Jim loved the music, and Lauryn said she really appreciated the pastor's exegesis of John 15.

After they snacked on food in the White House kitchen, the women went back to their brainstorming, and the President returned to the Oval Office. At 11:00 that evening, the women went back to the kitchen. They found Jim there already eating chocolate ice cream. They joined him.

Kathy returned to the airport and her flight back to San Francisco after breakfast on Monday morning. Lauryn and Ronnie took Kathy to the airport in an armored limo so that they could see her off. As they were driving back to the White House, Lauryn was deep in thought.

"Lauryn, you seem puzzled, for some reason."

She shook her head. "It's not that I'm puzzled. I have friends who might be able to help us with financing some research without involving the military."

"Really! Who?"

Lauryn shook her head. "I don't want to say their names unless they agree to a meeting. When we get back to the office, I need to talk to Phil Kaiser first."

Inside the White House, they had just gone past security. Down the hall, she spotted Phil Kaiser, and Lauryn caught his eye. "Excuse me, Phil, have you got a moment?"

He nodded. The other person who was with Phil excused herself. "What can I do for you?"

"This last weekend, I had a guest who stayed at the eDreams hotel."

He nodded. "Yes, Katheryn Suvari. What about her?"

"This is not about Kathy, but about eDreams. Does the hotel have a dining room where I can be reasonably certain of both security and privacy?"

He nodded. "Yes, we have used that hotel frequently. Do you need to make some arrangements?"

"Possibly. I'm going to talk to a man and his wife about coming to stay at the hotel and then meeting me for breakfast or lunch one day."

Phil nodded. "That can be arranged. Just let me know who it is and the day and time."

"Thank you, Phil."

He walked away, and Lauryn and Ronnie went on to the First Lady office suite. "Ronnie, I need some privacy while I make this call. If they say yes, I'll tell you all about it."

"Okay." As she went into the outer office, she closed the door behind her.

8.
Networking

Lauryn picked up the handset. "Operator, I need to talk with Casper and Diane Whirry in Malibu, California."

"I'll put you through when I reach them, Mrs. Smith."

A few minutes later, Lauryn's phone rang. She picked up the handset, and the operator said, "I have Casper and Diane Whirry on the line."

"Thank you. Casper! Diane! How are you?"

Casper responded first. "We're fine! It's great to hear from you, Lauryn. I talked with Jim a couple of weeks ago."

Diane jumped into the conversation. "Hi, Lauryn. It's good to hear your voice. What's up?"

"This past weekend was extraordinary, and I want to talk with both of you about it, but I want to see you too. How would you like to come to Washington and spend a couple of days at the eDreams, down the street from the White House?"

Diane was enthusiastic. "That would be great! We love that hotel! Not long ago we donated to the Smithsonian, so we could make a little side trip to see that new display."

Casper shared Diane's attitude. "We can fly out tomorrow and be there before dinner."

"That would be fine. Jim and I have other plans for dinner tomorrow, but I'd like to come and join you at the eDreams for either breakfast or lunch."

There was whispering in the background. Casper was upbeat. "We'll meet you for breakfast. We've heard about your Chief of Staff, Veronica Miller. If you want to bring her along, we'd like to meet her."

They couldn't see Lauryn smiling. "I'll invite her. I think she'd enjoy meeting you too. We'll see you Wednesday morning for breakfast."

"Okay. See you then." The call ended, and Lauryn pushed a button. "Come on in, Ronnie."

Her chief of staff came in and closed the door behind her. "Okay, what's the scoop?"

"On Wednesday morning, you and I are going to have breakfast with Casper and Diane Whirry."

Ronnie's mouth was agape. "The Whirrys? You've known them for a long time, haven't you?"

"Yes." Then, Lauryn told them the gist of the conversation. "After breakfast, Casper and Diane will go to the Smithsonian and spend the day there with the new exhibit. Sometime during our breakfast, the President will put a call through to Casper, telling him that he understands that Casper and his wife are in town for the exhibit, and would they like to come to dinner that evening."

Ronnie was impressed. "This way, the Whirrys are in town to see the Smithsonian exhibit. The media won't know that you and I met with them for breakfast, and you and the President will be with them for dinner. Cool!"

Lauryn nodded. "Between now and Wednesday morning, you and our staff need to set up a networking meeting at the U.N. building. Tomorrow, you and I will go to New York and spend most of the day. Arrange for a helicopter to pick you and me up and bring us back on the south lawn. I will talk to Phil about tomorrow. When I do, I'll also tell him about the breakfast, which will be in a secure dining room. Have our staff make phone calls today to recruit people for tomorrow's networking luncheon. I want you personally to call the three that met with me previously and connect with them, letting them know that you'll be with me tomorrow. There are some female ambassadors in town. See if some of their spouses can be included in the luncheon. You know how to do it."

Ronnie nodded. "I've got it. This will be a busy day, the beginning of another busy week."

"Right." As Ronnie left her office, Lauryn picked up her desk phone and pushed buttons for her husband's Chief of Staff. "Good morning, Jay, this is Lauryn."

"I'm calling you to let you know about a couple of things that are happening so that you can be aware of them. Please keep this under your hat except for my husband. I hope to have lunch with him today and update him. I need about five minutes of your time right now, okay?"

"Okay. Just a moment." He closed the door to his outer office. "What's up?" He sat down at his desk.

"Tomorrow I'm going back to New York for a networking meeting, and I'm taking Ronnie with me. A helicopter will pick us up on the South Lawn. These networking lunches only involve the Oval Office indirectly or obliquely."

"I understand."

"The other thing involves something that is strictly need-to-know. Tomorrow, publicly, the Smithsonian is opening a new display that has been financed by Casper and Diane Whirry. That is the official reason they are flying into Washington tomorrow and staying at the eDreams. My husband will call them and invite them to dinner in the White House residence for Wednesday evening. That dinner will also be public knowledge. So far, what I've told you will all be public knowledge."

"Okay, so what's the rest?"

"During the campaign, I was invited to Houston for a town meeting of scientists at the Johnson Space Center."

"I heard about that."

"Out of that meeting grew my greater friendship with Katheryn Suvari, the Director of Livermore National

Laboratory, who, as you know, visited here last weekend. That's no secret. What nobody knows except those of us who had dinner together last Friday evening – and now you – was the reason for Kathy's visit."

Lauryn then gave Jay an outline of the weekend's discussions. Then she told him, "So Ronnie and I will be having breakfast on Wednesday morning in a secured dining room at the eDreams, with Phil Kaiser and other agents on watch."

"Holy moley! This is huge!"

"I agree. If this initial effort fails, few people will ever know that the White House was in any way involved. If it succeeds, it might turn into a historical event."

"My notes of this conversation will be in a password-protected and secured file. I assume that you're taking the same precautions."

"That's right. You might want to mention to my husband that you and I had a confidential conversation regarding last weekend and some of this week."

"I'll plan on it, Lauryn. Thanks for bringing me up to speed."

"You're welcome. Let's get back to work." She ended the call.

Jay sat at his desk, silently stunned, for several minutes. He touched his intercom button. "Jane, the First Lady wants to have lunch with the President. Let's try to make it happen if we can."

"Okay."

In her office, Lauryn was thoughtful. She touched her intercom button. "Ronnie, call my husband's body man, Demarcus. Tell him I want to have lunch with my husband today, if at all possible."

"Okay."

It was a good thing they had lunch together. Jim did not return to the residence bedroom that night until after Lauryn was asleep. There were warning signs that the

Yellowstone Caldera might erupt for the first time in 630,000 years. If it erupted again, all life on Earth would be radically affected.

When the White House operator awakened him, Lauryn was already up, dressed, and having breakfast in their private dining room. She was finishing her juice and second up of tea when he came in and kissed her. "You're up early. What time will the helicopter pick you up for New York?"

She smiled. "Ronnie and I are supposed to leave at 9:30."

"Okay. Jay told me that you called him. He was astounded, and he's glad you're handling the project the way you are. I am too."

"We'll undoubtedly know much more tomorrow after Ronnie and I meet with Casper and Diane."

Jim nodded. "I agree. If Casper and Diane decide to get involved themselves, it could be financially risky for them in addition to being a physically dangerous project. You can tell them that I suggest we not involve the EPA unless it is absolutely necessary. If the research is done on one of the islands they own in the Pacific, the EPA can be kept out of the loop."

"I agree." She looked at her watch. "I need to get going. Ronnie will want to check in with me before we get close to leaving for New York." She got up from the table, kissed Jim briefly, and left.

As Lauryn walked into her office suite, Ronnie met her. "It appears there will be a total of twenty-two or twenty-three of us today." They walked together into Lauryn's office and shut the door. Ronnie continued to report. "We'll be in a slightly larger private conference room. Juliette called me this morning to say she and her husband will be flying home to Paris for at least a week today, and she expressed her regrets. Maria, Jillian, and

Margret will be with us, and Schultz will be our porter again."

"Good. We've got another forty-five minutes before the helicopter lands to pick us up. If you've got nothing else to report at the moment, I want to talk to Jason for a few minutes."

"Okay." Ronnie walked out.

A moment later, Jason came in. "You wanted to see me, Ma'am?"

"Yes, Jason, have a seat. This morning I was talking with Jay Fillion, and something he said made me think of you. He said his notes on our conversation would be kept in a secure password-protected file. As far as we're concerned here, the networking work that Ronnie and I are doing can be kept on our computers in a directory that is at least moderately secure."

"Yes, Ma'am, I'm following our federal security protocols."

Lauryn nodded. "That's fine. I'm sure Ronnie has kept all of you up to date on our other major project as well. She has emphasized to you how important it is to keep a tight lid on what is happening in our fusion energy project."

"Yes, Ma'am." He smiled warmly. "She's put the fear of God into us."

"Good." Lauryn paused. "I want you to create the tightest possible security you can do for the fusion energy project. I want it much tighter than any federal protocols. You can do this, can't you?"

"Yes, Ma'am, it will be a nice challenge."

"Jason, if you create a back door, I want you to give me the key and then forget where the door is."

He smiled broadly. "I can do ever better than that, Ma'am! After I get everything set up, I'll explain it to you."

"Good, Jason, go to it!"

He got up and left. She went to a sidebar in her office and got a couple of energy bars out of a hidden refrigerator.

She also opened a small bottle of chocolate soy milk and began to drink. She put the energy bars in her purse, and then she went to the window of her office and looked out.

"Lord, every morning I've been asking you to use me on your terms your way. I trust you with everything. If I'm inadvertently making a mess, I pray you'll help me clean it up later." She took several minutes to be simply present to God's presence, and then she prayed silently for a while without moving a muscle.

There was a soft knock at her door, and Ronnie came in. "It's time, Lauryn."

"Okay, let's go."

Inside the helicopter, Ronnie looked around. She was impressed, as Lauryn had been her first time. "I've always wondered about the insides of these things." The engines started, but things remained relatively quiet. "I know this is simply part of your job, but I'm impressed."

Their Secret Service chief nodded. "I understand."

Just over an hour later, when they walked into the conference room, it reminded Lauryn of joining a reception at her church. There were groups of two or three engaged in conversations scattered all over the room. There were two men drinking coffee off to her right, and Lauryn headed for them. "Good morning, gentlemen, I'm Lauryn Smith, First Lady of the United States."

The taller of the two introduced himself. "I recognized you, ma'am, and I'm delighted to meet you. I'm Stanley Palmer, husband of Dame Helen Palmer, the Prime Minister of New Zealand."

The other man nodded and smiled. "I too am glad to meet you, Mrs. Smith. I am Paul Girard, life partner of Kevin Costello, the Prime Minister of Australia."

It took nearly an hour for Lauryn and Ronnie to greet the thirty-one spouses of world leaders. Several of them joined the luncheon out of curiosity because most of them knew Juliette Debré, Maria Cedronio, Jillian Wright, or

Margret Thors, the women who had attended the first meeting.

Lauryn spoke quietly to Schultz, and then she went and stood at the end of a large, oblong table that was surrounded with chairs. "Ladies and Gentlemen, good morning again to all of you! It has taken a bit longer than expected for Ronnie Miller and me to greet all of you. Ronnie is my Chief of Staff at the White House. Let's all sit down, and lunch will be served to us in a few minutes."

During the luncheon, Lauryn and Ronnie took turns talking about the network being formed as they ate. Casual conversations continued into the middle of the afternoon when some of them began to say farewell. The helicopter returned, took the back to Washington, and landed on the south lawn of the White House as the sun was setting.

Seeing cameras and microphones set up next to the edge of the landing area, Lauryn and Ronnie walked over there. Just before they reached the small podium that was set up, the President came out of the Oval Office to greet them. He embraced Lauryn and greeted Ronnie with a handshake.

Jim whispered to Lauryn, so she went to the microphone first. "Good afternoon everyone. My Chief of Staff and I have spent most of the day at the United Nations building, meeting with the significant others of several of our world's leaders. We did not meet officially, but as friends. It has been enjoyable getting to know one another and share lunch together." She stepped slightly to one side, and Jim came and stood beside her, with his arm around her.

"I'm glad that my wife is nurturing these friendships. Some of the people she saw today have been friends of ours for years because of her travels with her previous work. Our United Nations Ambassador, Amber Heigl, is being kept informed if any developments might appear."

Lauryn leaned over. "I'm hoping to have another luncheon such as this one today in a few months. Are there any questions?" She pointed.

"John Andrews, UNN. Why was this meeting set up?"

Lauryn smiled. "As I said, we've known some of these people many years. We met Juliette Debré, wife of the French Ambassador, for instance, when he was Prime Minister of France many years ago. Genuine friendships, even political ones, are worth maintaining. I'll take one more question." She pointed again.

"Corrine Rogers, PBS. You mentioned Juliette Debré, who is known for working with sick children in France. Do you think she would be interested in making an appearance on one of our children's shows?"

Lauryn smiled broadly. "She and her husband are at home in Paris this week. She was not with us today. I'll be glad to ask her when she returns to New York." She looked at Jim, and he nodded slightly. "That's all for today. I hope dinner is waiting for us because I'm starving."

There was scattered laughter as people began moving away. Jim spoke quietly. "Ronnie, you're welcome to join us for dinner if you like."

"Thank you! That will be great!"

They went towards the White House and turned towards the entrance to the residence. The Cornish game hens were enjoyable as usual. Jim enjoyed hearing about old friends that had come to the luncheon. He was also fascinated by what he learned about Stanley Palmer from New Zealand, and Paul Girard from Australia. At the time, New Zealand was behaving as a true ally for the United States. Australia's Prime Minister had been critical of Jim when he first became President, but most of their points at issue were being resolved.

9.
Science Challenges

Lauryn and Ronnie were having some Earl Grey tea in the little dining room at eDreams when the Whirrys arrived. Lauryn put her cup down and greeted them. "Good morning, Diane! Good morning, Casper!"

"Good morning Lauryn!" They responded together. As she hugged Lauryn, she asked, "Is the Secret Service guarding the door for a reason?"

Lauryn smiled. "They are who they are. Casper, Diane, this is Veronica Miller, my Chief of Staff. Everyone calls her Ronnie."

Ronnie was thrilled to meet the billionaires. "Good morning to you both. I'm glad to meet you at last!" She shook their hands.

Casper nodded. "Several times we have been in the same place at the same time, but we've never met." He turned to Lauryn. "Diane and I are looking forward to hearing about the extraordinary weekend you mentioned."

"We'll get to that. Let's order our breakfasts, and after the wait staff has delivered it, we can talk about it."

They all sat down, and when Lauryn pressed a small button beside her water glass, a waiter came in and took their orders. They made small talk until the food came, and Lauryn said to the waiter, "That will be all until after we leave." He nodded.

Lauryn said a prayer, and as they began eating Lauryn began their presentation. "Just over a year ago, during the campaign, I was asked to be part of a town meeting at the

Johnson Space Center in Houston. In attendance were scientists from all over the country were there. The idea was, if I became First Lady, I could use the position for the advancement of real science over the pseudo-science that predominates so much of politics and the Internet."

Diane looked up. "Pseudoscience?"

Ronnie nodded. "Some people call it Junk Science."

Lauryn continued as they ate. "Ainsley Schafer, Tours Director of the Johnson Space Center, led off the discussion. She said that many of the questions they are asked during their tours arise out of what is often described as pseudo-science. The Internet seems to encourage its rapid growth, dwarfing legitimate scientific developments."

Casper nodded. "That's certainly true."

"One particular suggestion caught my attention more than the others. Katheryn Suvari, the Director of Livermore National Laboratory, made a comment while talking about something else. She pointed out that most of the scientists there recognized that there is an overwhelming difference between nuclear fission and nuclear fusion, but no one is interested in pursuing the difference technologically because of the distractions of pseudo-science. Kathy was with us last weekend."

Ronnie took over because Lauryn's food was getting cold. "We don't know how familiar you are with that subject. I'll briefly explain while Lauryn eats. "Fusion energy and fission energy are opposites. Fission comes when splitting an atom. It is commonly used to power nuclear plants and weapons. Fusion occurs constantly on the surface of our sun, where most of the sun's energy comes from, by way of the fusion of hydrogen into helium atoms. That makes a heavier nucleus and produces a little leftover energy because when those nuclei fuse, they create energy."

Diane nodded. "So, it happens on the sun, but not on earth?"

Ronnie nodded. "It only happens in laboratories. Fusion does not produce runaway chain reactions, so there can't be a meltdown. Fusion reactions do not produce much radioactive waste either. The challenge is, for fusion to occur here on Earth, we need a temperature of 180 million degrees Fahrenheit—six times hotter than the sun's core."

Casper put his fork down. "So last weekend, you two, in conversations with Katheryn Suvari, were talking about taking something impossible and making it technologically possible and practical, if I'm getting where you're going with this."

Lauryn nodded. "That is the gist of it. The main barrier to generating energy through a fusion reaction is usually defined in terms of getting government funding. Each time there's talk about climate change, funding for it rises on this subject for a while, but there has never been enough funding to get the first power plants built. For less than $50 billion, we could build a working reactor, but it would probably not be at all dependable. Our question becomes now whether we can make it both trustworthy and affordable." Lauryn remembered saying this to her husband on Friday night's dinner.

Ronnie continued Lauryn's point. "Here's the challenge as we are redefining it."

Casper stared at Ronnie and Lauryn. "You're redefining the challenge?"

Lauryn smiled, and Ronnie nodded. "Yes, sir. Fusion reactions can occur here on Earth inside tokamaks, which are doughnut-shaped chambers where inert gas is pumped into a vacuum chamber and electricity flows through the center. The gas is charged, making plasma that is locked inside the chamber by magnetic fields. Radio and microwaves are fired into the plasma to raise its temperature, and at the right temperature, fusion occurs. The barrier to a sustained reaction, other than the high cost of the electricity to start this, has previously been finding a material that can withstand that much heat for more than a few seconds. We think there's a way around that."

Now it was Diane's turn to stare. "How do you get around a temperature of 180 million degrees?"

Lauryn had finished her breakfast, so she pushed her plate aside and picked up her cup of tea. "Instead of trying to develop a material that can withstand that temperature constantly, we think there's a way technologically to provide a buffer between the fusion reaction and the material of that container. It's called the Leidenfrost effect. Above a liquid's boiling point, the effect produces an insulating vapor layer. This was discussed years ago on an episode of *Mythbusters*, broadcast by PBS. We are initially talking about liquid tungsten flowing over the solid material of the container on the inside, while injecting tungsten powder into the plasma with the other ingredients. That continuously changing vapor might provide the needed Leidenfrost effect Ronnie is talking about."

Ronnie was also finished with her breakfast. "Researching and developing this technology is physically dangerous as well as probably expensive. If it works, it will be revolutionary. If the EPA were to get involved during the research, they could bring it to a halt."

Casper sat there with his mouth slightly open for almost a minute. "Lauryn, as Diane can tell you, over the decades, she and I have been together, I've only been surprised by something twice." He looked at his wife, and she nodded. "This is only the third time, and I never dreamed, Lauryn, that you would be someone who could overwhelm me with such a surprise."

Diane nodded, grinning. "Amen to that! Me too!"

"Like you said, Ronnie, if it works, it will be truly revolutionary. Diane and I need to pray about it. I'm sure that we can help get this research done, but how to help get it done is the question. Since Katheryn Suvari lives in the San Francisco area, it won't be hard to create an opportunity to meet with her. I've had dealings with the Lawrence Livermore National Laboratory on more than one occasion over the years. I'm familiar with what they do. I'm not surprised at her interest and involvement in this."

Lauryn nodded. "I hope you'll have at least one opportunity to meet her. Kathy and I are becoming good friends. I think you'll like her."

Casper and Diane had many questions, and Lauryn and Ronnie were prepared for the questions. When they said good-bye to Casper and Diane as they were going back to their suite, Lauryn looked at Ronnie. "I think we're on the right track, don't you?"

Ronnie nodded. "Yes, I'll be interested to hear tomorrow about any of your conclusions after you have dinner with them tonight."

Lauryn nodded. "Let's get back to the office."

Phil Kaiser had an SUV waiting for them in front of eDreams, so they were walking into Lauryn's office suite a few minutes later. Jason looked up from his desk. "Good morning! Someone tried to hack into our secured files, and I've already reported it to security." He looked directly at Lauryn. "Maria Cedronio wants you to call her, Ma'am."

Lauryn nodded. She went into her office and closed the door behind her. Taking the secure phone from her purse, she quickly selected Maria from her contacts. "Good morning, Maria! This is Lauryn Smith."

"Good morning!"

"I just got back from a breakfast meeting. I was told you called."

"Yes, thank you for returning my call." She spoke softly and conspiratorially. "At the press conference this morning, the White House Press Secretary mentioned yesterday's terrorist attack in Malta. My husband has prepared a speech strongly condemning the attack for a press conference this afternoon. I have information for Amber Heigl, your Ambassador, if she and I can accidentally meet in the ladies' room at the Visitors' Center. I know she is here today, so I'd like to meet with her at about fifteen minutes before noon."

Lauryn was jotting notes quickly on her scratch pad. "Maria, I'll do my best to make it happen."

"Grazie! Thank you, Lauryn. I must go." The connection ended.

Lauryn touched an intercom button. "Marnette, come in, please."

The young woman came in. "Yes, Ma'am?"

"Go over into the other West Wing offices and find a place where you can casually make a quick phone call."

"From one of their phones?"

"Yes. It doesn't matter whose phone you use, but the call must not come from our offices. Call Amber Heigl. She's in New York. Try her office at the U.N. first. Tell her that Maria Cedronio, the wife of Italy's Ambassador wants to meet her accidentally in the ladies' room at the Visitor Center at 11:45 this morning. Got it?"

Marnette nodded. "Yes, Ma'am."

"After you've delivered the message, come straight back here and go on with whatever you were doing when I called you."

"Yes, Ma'am." She turned and left.

Lauryn leaned back in her chair and was thoughtful. There was a soft knock at her door, and Phil came in.

"We've traced that attempted hack of your server. It was by someone we've encountered before. You needn't be worried at this point. At our request, the C.I.A. has already tested the strength of your security protocols. You have virtually no risk. The C.I.A. tried to hire Jason three years ago after he exposed some weaknesses in their systems. Jason Pounds is one of the best there is. You can be glad Ronnie hired him."

"Thank you, Phil."

"Okay." He turned and left.

A few minutes later, Lauryn's desk phone rang. Caller ID identified the caller as Amber Heigl. "Good morning!"

"Good morning, Lauryn. I just got your message from Marnette. She said she was calling from one of the phone lines of the Press Secretary."

"Good."

"Did Maria give you any details?"

"No, she seemed to be in a hurry, but it sounded important. Knowing Maria as I do, I think she probably wants to brief you on what her husband is going to say at his press conference because you may be asked by the media about the attack."

"Okay, thank you. We'll be in touch, right?"

"Right." They ended the call. She pushed a button. "Ronnie?" Her chief of staff came in and sat down. "Did Marnette tell you what I had her do?"

Ronnie nodded slightly. "Yes. It appears the network has started to function."

"Yes. Tell Marnette that passing messages like this could become almost routine. Confidentiality is important, so this is our business, and it's not to be shared with others in the West Wing."

"Okay. I'll debrief her on what she did, and she and I will discuss possible improvements or some possible variations in the routine. Jay called. He said you and the Whirrys are to meet for dinner at 7:00."

"Okay." She looked at the grandfather clock in the corner. "This is going to be another long day."

Dinner conversations were light that evening until they had finished their fresh fruit cups and were served broiled halibut steaks. Casper was relaxed and almost mellow. "Lauryn, it would be helpful if you can have a few of your scientist friends call me. Who, besides Katheryn Suvari, are those most likely be interested in innovations regarding fusion research?"

Lauryn nodded. "I'll give it some thought, and I'll be talking again with Katheryn." She continued talking as she ate. "Do either of you know Kevin Costello, the Prime Minister of Australia?"

Diane smiled. "We know him. He seems to be an effective leader and more honest than most."

"That's what his partner, Paul Girard, told me one day. Isn't there a fusion research facility down under?"

"Hmm." Casper was thoughtful. "Diane, let's find out what they're doing right now down there. It might be a place to begin. Probably the most research thus far has been in Northern Germany and Southern France. I admit that I don't know how much they are accomplishing in Australia, but I think Kevin Costello is someone we can work with."

Diane nodded. "Since Casper and I have decided to explore this, we're going to avoid the limelight for a while. We can communicate through the private channels we've used since your governorship in California. Otherwise, we'll stay out of sight."

Two months later, Casper and Diane endowed a research project in Southern France. The media discussed fusion research for over a week. The media were not aware, however, of another endowed research project that began in Australia.

That was the last time that Lauryn and the President saw or heard from Casper and Diane for more than two years. The midterm elections resulted in almost half of the incumbents running were not re-elected. In some cases, the ones not re-elected had been very vocal in their opposition to James Smith for President two years earlier.

When Kevin Costello and his partner, Paul Girard, came for dinner in late March, Casper Whirry was mentioned only in passing. Jim and Lauryn emphasized the strong alliance between Australia and the U.S. They discussed mutual ecological challenges, and Prime Minister Costello expressed his appreciation for Lauryn's helping

Paul connect with other countries through Lauryn's network.

A week later, Juliette Debré called Lauryn. After exchanging pleasantries, Juliette got to the gist of her call. "My husband Paul and I always enjoy seeing images in the news when the cherry trees are blossoming around the tidal basin. Could we impose upon you to show us the best views of the trees?"

"It would be no imposition at all, Juliette. When would you two be able to come?" Lauryn was very fond of her, and this would be another opportunity to feed their friendship.

"Would tomorrow afternoon be too soon?"

"Not at all! Have your limo bring you and your Ambassador husband to the White House. I will check with my husband to see if they can meet briefly, and then we'll take a tour of the tidal basin."

"Trés bon! Excellent! We will see you tomorrow!"

As they ended the call, Lauryn touched an intercom button. "Ronnie, call my husband's body man, Demarcus. I need to talk with either him or Jay Fillion. Jay would be better if he's available. I need to talk with one of them ASAP!"

Less than a minute later, Lauryn's phone rang, and she looked at the caller ID. "Good morning, Jay!"

"Good morning, Lauryn. What's up?"

"I just had a call from Juliette Debré, the wife of Paul Debré, France's ambassador to the U.N. She asked me to give her and her husband a tour of the cherry blossoms around the tidal basin. I think there may be more to this than the tour."

"Really!"

"Two possibilities occur to me, Jay. If my husband has the time, he could join us in a brief tour. The other possibility is to set aside a block of time in the evening when the Ambassador and his wife can be with us for dinner and conversations." Lauryn could hear papers rustling in the background.

"This is interesting, Lauryn. The President and I were discussing France earlier this morning." He paused. "I can rearrange the schedule for tomorrow. We'll do what has to be done before lunch, and the President will have the rest of the day free."

"Thanks, Jay. Ronnie and I will do the same thing here. I'll see you tomorrow if not before."

"Right."

They ended the call. Lauryn yelled. "Ronnie!"

She came in the door. "Yes?"

"If I have anything on my schedule tomorrow after lunch, reschedule it." Lauryn went on to tell Ronnie what was now on the agenda. Then she told Ronnie to close the door and sit down, which she did.

Ronnie spoke calmly. "Do you think this has anything to do with Casper and Diane's work in Southern France?"

"I don't have a clue. I told Jay that I thought there is something more to this visit than seeing the cherry blossoms. Jay told me that he and the President were talking about France earlier this morning. I haven't seen anything in the news about France in the last several weeks, have you?"

"No, but when we were talking with Katheryn two weeks ago, I remember her saying that there seems to be more progress taking place in Southern France than in Australia."

Lauryn nodded. "I remember. Let's hustle up and try not to leave anything for tomorrow that can't wait until later in the week."

"Right." Ronnie got up and left.

Lauryn's desk phone rang again with another call from Jay. "The President and I have a full day tomorrow, but we'll make sure that after 4:00 the evening is free. I called the chef to let him know there will be guests for dinner. I suggest that you call Juliette Debré and tell here they are invited to dinner. They can spend the night in the Lincoln Bedroom."

Lauryn smiled. "I'll make the call right now." She ended that call, took out her secure cell, and called New York. "Juliette! The afternoon is cleared for touring the tidal basin's cherry trees as well as any other sites you or your husband want to see. Then, you and your husband are invited to the White House residence dining room to have dinner with my husband and me. You're also invited to spend the night in the Lincoln Bedroom if you wish."

"Trés bon! Excellent! Wonderful! I'm sure my husband will be most pleased! Bien! We will see you tomorrow!"

That evening, Lauryn and Jim discussed the situation extensively. "France was in my security briefing this morning, yet the Ambassador's wife calls you to arrange a meeting. We can be sure this is a way to work around diplomatic channels. We can only wonder why."

Lauryn was thoughtful. "We've known Paul and Juliette for more than twenty years. We can all remember our first meeting in Paris when I introduced Sony's newest cameras, both still and professional video cameras. Ronnie and I discussed the possibility that this is about something that Casper and Diane are financing."

"I guess we'll find out tomorrow. Juliette called me back just before I left the office on my secure phone to say everything is set."

"Good."

Steaming bowls of soup were brought in, so they sat down to dinner.

10.
Blossoms & Boldness

Lauryn had just finished lunch with her staff in her office when they were notified that Juliette and Paul Debré had arrived earlier than expected and wanted to meet Lauryn in her office. The Chief Usher, David Garner, was called. Lauryn met them at the elevator near her suite. "Paul! Juliette!" She hugged them both. "Welcome! My staff would like to meet you!"

The Ambassador nodded. "Juliette wanted me to see where you work. This is genuinely nice."

"Thank you." Lauryn led them to her staff, who were standing nearby in a semi-circle. She made the introductions. Then she took them into her office, which had been thoroughly straightened and dusted during the previous five minutes. "Please make yourselves comfortable. Ronnie will bring us coffee and scones in a moment."

They sat down, and Juliette was obviously excited. "When I did that show for PBS, I enjoyed it very much, but this is so much more exciting! I have been fascinated with pictures and stories of this White House since I was a little girl."

Her husband nodded. "I think one of the reasons she wanted me to take her to see the cherry blossoms was so that we could also see the White House. In France, we have a long history and many historic buildings, but this building survives from the earliest years of these United States. It has a fascinating history."

Lauryn smiled warmly for her old friends. "This evening, after dinner, I'll be happy to show you as much as you would like to see before you retire. Your overnight luggage has been placed in the Lincoln Bedroom for you."

Paul nodded. "After we tour the trees around your tidal basin, I hope we can pause to spend some time at your Lincoln and Jefferson memorials. In my teen years, I read biographies of both men. I read the entire six-volume set of Mr. Lincoln by Carl Sandburg."

Juliette smiled. "Since we have become relocated to New York, we have been reading newer biographies of them."

Ronnie came in, served coffee, and left. For about an hour they chatted before they were escorted by Phil Kaiser to an escorted limousine. They made a full circuit of the tidal basin before they stopped at the Jefferson Memorial.

Standing at the bottom of the steps, they looked all around. Juliette murmured, "It's neoclassical architecture done in this perfect marble is stunning!"

Paul nodded. "Beautiful!" They started up the steps, with Lauryn behind them. The Secret Service and Capitol Police kept the crowd back without blocking access to the Memorial.

Standing at the top and close to the statue, Paul read one of the inscriptions aloud.

> We hold these truths to be self-evident: that all men are created equal, that they are endowed by their Creator with certain inalienable rights, among these are life, liberty, and the pursuit of happiness, that to secure these rights governments are instituted among men. We... solemnly publish and declare, that these colonies are and of right ought to be free and independent states ... And for the support of this declaration, with a firm reliance on the protection of divine providence, we mutually pledge our lives, our fortunes, and our sacred honor.

The Ambassador's eyes grew wider. "I had never noticed in any of his biographies! Fascinating!"

Lauren smiled. "What's fascinating, Paul?"

"In your Declaration of Independence, which he wrote, he used the phrase, 'unalienable rights.' Here, Jefferson is quoted as saying 'inalienable rights.' I must study this! I must consult an English-French dictionary."

Juliette shook her head. "I never noticed it either."

They stayed almost an hour, discussing both the inscriptions on the inside of the memorial and the nineteen-foot tall bronze statue. Then they got back into the limousine for a drive to the Lincoln Memorial.

There, standing with his arm around Juliette, Ambassador Debré had tears running down his cheeks. "I don't think any other leader in our world's history struggled and suffered for his country more, and yet he demonstrated more dignity and grace amid his country's tragic civil war than anyone else either." He and his wife took in the entire look of the complex before they started up the steps and spent another hour there. Silently, Lauryn resolved to ask them about their impressions of the memorials over dinner that evening.

Juliette requested that they continue to see more of the city before heading back to the White House. Phil Kaiser knew by radio that the President needed another thirty minutes, so the tour was fitted into that time frame.

Jim met them in the Oval Office. After they greeted one another, this time it was Juliette's turn to stare more than her husband at their surroundings. "I know those large windows face south, so that door" (she pointed to her left) must go to the rose garden. I memorized this when I was a little girl. That door, then (she pointed to her right) must go to your private study and dining room. Am I right?"

Jim nodded. "You have a good memory. There are so many doors, it is easy to get them confused."

Paul grinned. "Your office is certainly designed to be intimidating, isn't it?"

Jim returned his smile. "That it is." We can sit down and talk here, Paul, but I think Juliette might prefer that Lauryn and I give you a tour."

Juliette's smile filled her face. Trés bien! Yes!"

As expected, there were tourists who stared at them, and Jim greeted a few of them. Lauryn led the way with Juliette. They ended up in the living room of the residence and sat down. After they had been served beverages, Jim told a security agent that they were not to be disturbed.

He had questions. "When Juliette called Lauryn and told her you wanted a tour of the cherry blossoms, we knew that there was probably more to your request than a tour. Furthermore, my security briefing yesterday morning included France."

Paul Debré nodded solemnly. "When the four of us first met two decades ago we were transparent with one another. I'm glad that this hasn't changed. France needs your help, probably unofficially, with the work one of your citizens is sponsoring in southern France. His name is Casper Whirry."

Jim nodded, and Juliette smiled and spoke. "We've known Casper and his wife, Diane, for many years. It was the Whirrys that helped propel my husband to the governorship of California, and more recently, they most generously contributed to our campaign for the Presidency."

Juliette nodded. "We know this. Madame Whirry told me that you told them that my husband and I could be trusted unconditionally, so they told us, in secret – no, no, -- in confidence about the fusion project and his initial involvement with financing further research at our fusion research laboratory in southern France. They also told us they were investing significantly in similar research in Australia and in two other locations."

Jim smiled warmly. "I'm glad they took you into their confidence. How is it that you are asking for my help?

Lauryn and I have not heard from Casper and Diane for many months."

The Ambassador nodded. "I asked them about that, and they said that they wanted to be careful to keep politicians away from becoming involved in any country. You have met the current Prime Minister of France, Christian Delmas. He and I have had some long talks about keeping politics away from scientific research as much as possible."

Lauryn spoke firmly. "When I have talked with other scientists, we all agree on this. May we assume that you have come up with a way for us to help? You said a moment ago that France needs our help, 'probably unofficially.' That's an interesting phrase."

Juliette smiled. "My husband made a suggestion to our Premiere, and he concurred."

Now Jim was fascinated. "It sounds like you want to engage in a completely legal conspiracy."

The Ambassador laughed. "Yes! Exactly! I'm suggesting that you openly call Prime Minister Delmas and arrange war games for our countries. The Chairman of your Joint Chiefs of Staff would arrange it as soon as possible with his counterpart in France. Monsieur Delmas will want it to be in the fifty kilometers surrounding the fusion laboratory. The war games can go on intermittently for three years, which is the block of time that the Whirrys say they need to complete what their current work there."

Jim nodded. "By doing this, our two countries will be providing security for the lab and its environment." He looked up at the ceiling. "I like it! I can get this started in a matter of hours. What do you think, Lauryn?"

She was thoughtful. "I think that the military needs to know what kind of research is going on in that lab, but they don't need to know the reasons for these war games at this time and in this place. Our Chairman of the Joint Chiefs should know for the United States. What about France?"

Paul nodded. "It can be arranged that way. Prime Minister Delmas can even make a light-hearted comment that for a short time, the laboratory will have the best possible security, or something to that effect."

The next morning, after Juliette and Paul Debré had left, Lauryn and Ronnie went out to an early lunch at Old Ebbitt Grill. Lauryn set up a conference call on her private cell phone with Ronnie, Katherine, and Brittany. "My daughter, you and I are going to need to talk about the reception in June. Right now, will you please mute your phone, ignore it for a half hour, and then hang up?"

"Okay, Mom." It was a mother-daughter strategy that had used with each other previously.

When Brittany's phone went silent, Lauryn talked to the scientists. "I've set this conference call on my private cell, but the usual boundaries should be kept." Lauryn then continued by carefully summarizing the conversations during the previous evening. She didn't use the word fusion, but instead referred to scientific research generically. She did not mention Casper or Diane by name. She also didn't mention the legal conspiracy.

Katherine was enthusiastic. She carefully responded to Lauryn's report, and then she said, "I'm so glad that you are able to influence scientific research from your position, Lauryn. It is everything we hoped for in our conference in Houston nearly three years ago. You and Ronnie enjoy your lunch. I ate at that grill once. I love it. We'll talk again soon."

Lauryn and Ronnie finished their lunches and went back to the office. Lauryn spoke quietly. "If anyone asks about my using my personal phone, I needed to talk to Brittany anyway. She and her fiancé, Mason, are having a small private wedding in June, and we're going to put on a White House reception for the happy couple."

"There's not going to be a White House wedding?"

Lauryn shook her head. "It's not something they want. It's not their style. They will be able to tell their children that they slept in the Lincoln Bedroom, though."

Ronnie smiled. "If I had a chance for a wedding here, I'd jump for it!" She paused. "While you were doing your tour yesterday, we got phone calls from Jillian Wright and from Margret Thors. I had Marnette follow our routine and pass on the messages to Amber Heigl. Last night, we got a text from Stanley Palmer. Marnette is handling that right now."

Lauryn nodded. "Good. The network is functioning just as I hoped. Each time we pass on information to Amber, we end up strengthening both the network and our country's ties with those countries." Lauryn didn't know what was actually happening while she spoke.

That evening, Lauryn and Jim were eating dinner when his phone rang. "Yes, Jay?"

"John Andrews is interviewing Amber Heigl on UNN. You and Lauryn might want to see it."

"Okay." He put away his phone and stood up. "Amber is being interviewed on UNN. Jay said we should watch."

Lauryn stood up. "The living room?"

"Yeah."

They went in and turned on a big video monitor. "Ambassador Heigl, it seems you are very popular with many people at the U.N. Were you surprised when Ambassador Cedronio made that speech about you?"

"Yes! It caught me completely off guard. I know the Ambassador from Italy, of course, but he and I have not spoken to each other in months."

As the interview went on, John Andrews referred to other ambassadors he had interviewed in the previous few weeks. There were brief clips of interviews with the ambassadors from New Zealand, Iceland, and the United Kingdom.

When Lauryn and Jim returned to their dining room, their wait staff was waiting. "Mr. President, we have taken your plates because the food had gotten cold. Would you like servings of the same thing again?"

Jim looked at Lauryn, and she responded. "Yes, please. We both love spareribs, and they're delicious."

They sat down again, and fresh servings were brought in. Lauryn ate a rib and sipped some coffee before she spoke. "I know you're keeping tabs on what's going on in the House and Senate. After the midterms brought more non-partisans into both chambers, do you think it has made a difference in the dynamics of how they work?"

"Without question, there's a difference. There's definitely less open divisiveness. Yes, the Democrats still have a majority in the House, and the Republicans still have a strong majority in the Senate, but the Independents are initiating more of the dialogue, and neither party has gotten used to it."

"Are you going to use Adam Paxton again when you run for re-election?"

He grinned. "Are you reading my mind? We haven't talked about my running again, but you're assuming I will." He winked at her.

"How long have we known each other? We routinely finish each other's sentences. We almost *do* read each other's minds!"

He half shrugged. "You're right about that, and about running for re-election. As for Adam Paxton, what do you think?"

Lauryn was thoughtful. "If he's available, Adam is undoubtedly our best choice. We know him, and he knows us. It also helps that he's just about the best there is."

Jim drank more coffee. "I'll talk to Jay about it tomorrow, and then I'll have him call Adam."

"Good.

11.
Developments

"I hope you'll forgive me, Mr. President, but I pretty well assumed you would run for re-election. In my mind, the odds were at least five to one in favor of it." Adam Paxton was relaxed as Jim, Jay, Lauryn, and Adam were conversing in the Oval Office.

Jim smiled. "I think my beloved wife knew it before I did."

Lauryn shook her head. "I assumed it, just as Adam did."

Jay spoke positively. "You won't be able to be on the road as much as you were the first time, but now you have what Teddy Roosevelt first called 'the bully pulpit.'"

The President ran his hand through his hair, which was now slightly streaked with grey. "Adam, I want you to select Senate and House seats carefully that I can support either with mentions in press conferences or with strategic visits. Those visits should also coincide with political issues, and I prefer to help those in the political middle."

Adam nodded. "Based upon what happened three years ago, you're probably going to gain some friends and supporters this time around. By the way, I was talking with Alfred Wells the other day."

Lauryn gazed at Adam incredulously. "The director that Jim scored three movies for?"

Jim smiled. "Four."

Adam nodded. "That's the one. He said that if you want to fly out to Burbank, he'll set up a fundraiser for you."

Lauryn turned to Jim. "Didn't you score that last movie you did with him in the style of Miklós Rózsa? You did that after you and I went to the old Odeon Leicester Square art deco theater and saw a screening of *El Cid*, didn't you?"

Jim nodded. "I could watch that movie again and still once again.""

Adam nodded. "The *El Cid* score was good, but I think the Miklós Rózsa score for the 1950s version of *Ben Hur* was better." He paused. "That's beside the point. Once you do a fund-raiser with Alfred Wells and all the other celebrities who will show up for it, I doubt you'll need to do other fundraisers this second time around. He and Julie can make things happen in Southern California. In some ways, Julie is even more influential than he is."

Lauryn nodded. "Jim, why don't you let me do this. I've got an idea for how the network can be helpful to Julie and Al. I'll call Julie tomorrow morning."

Her husband nodded. "I trust your judgment on that."

Adam was genuinely curious. "What's this about a network?"

Lauryn now spoke calmly and evenly to Adam. "The network is not something that wants media attention for itself. When I was representing Sony, everywhere we went, we made friends with politicians, and most of them had friendships with directors and producers. Jim and I made connections with all of them. Many of the spouses of some of the most influential people in every country are on the network. If Julie connects with the spouses of producers and directors elsewhere, they can create a positive and supportive buzz for Jim's re-election."

Adam whistled. "Be sure you don't overdo it."

With the three-hour time difference, Lauryn waited until almost noon the next morning before calling Julie on her office phone and made it a video call. As usual, Julie was effervescent. "Lauryn! I was hoping I'd hear from you!"

"Good morning, Julie! Someone told me that you and Al want to do a fundraiser for us. That's the main reason I'm calling this morning."

"Excellent! How soon can the President work it into his schedule?"

"I talked with Jay Fillion, my husband's Chief of Staff, last evening. A fundraiser for Paul Wilson is planned for next Saturday, the 28th, in Sacramento. Jim and I would like to worship on Sunday morning at our old home church in Long Beach, so we'll be in the area. What do you think?"

"Let me think." She was silent less than ten seconds. "I'll make it happen, Lauryn. I'll have the details in a few days. What was the other reason you were calling?"

"This is strictly just between you and me, okay?"

"Strictly private, no gossip, I swear."

Lauryn took about ten minutes to explain how her network developed, and how it had been working through the United Nations. Then she went on. "Julie, my network can help you create a network with the wives or husbands of producers and directors everywhere. That could be profitable for you and Al, and maybe you and I can help each other."

"Lauryn! Why didn't I think of this before?! It's brilliant, my friend! You and I are both going to have to keep our networks behind the scenes. I love this!"

"I can suggest a starting point for you, Julie."

"Who?"

"When I first got started with Sony, I went to Paris, and Jim went with me. That's when Jim finalized arrangements for writing the score for the biopic on Claude Debussy. You may remember that the film got an Oscar for part of Debussy's *La Cathedrale Engoulte* being played as a gothic cathedral rose out of the ocean."

"I remember that!" Julie smiled. "They played about five minutes of it during the Oscars presentation on that giant screen in the Walt Disney Theater. Jim's score led the audience into the scene. It was so powerful, Al and I had tears running down our cheeks!"

Lauryn also smiled. "The producer of that film is a woman. Her name is Tonie Dauphin. She's a sweetheart. Have you ever met her?"

"No, but I've heard of her."

"When you call her, tell her about this conversation. She speaks almost flawless English. Juliette Debré, the wife of the French Ambassador to the U.S., is a good friend of hers too."

"Okay. I should be able to tell you by the day-after tomorrow where we'll hold the fundraiser on the weekend. That'll give me four days to make things happen for the fundraiser. It'll be a little tight, but I can do it. I'll call you when I have it set up. Shall I use this number you're using now?"

Lauryn nodded. "When you call this number, you'll get the White House switchboard. Just ask for my office. If I'm not in the office, just ask for Ronnie. She's my Chief of Staff."

"Okay! See you soon!"

They nodded to each other and ended the call.

Jim began the re-election process with Adam Paxton the next day. Among the Republicans and Democrats, candidates who were solidly in the political middle began to emerge. The primaries would sort them out. After keynoting the major fundraiser for Paul Wilson, Air Force One flew them south to the Long Beach Airport, where they spent the night at the Best Western Plus at the Convention Center.

For Lauryn and Jim, the next morning felt like stepping back in time. The musicians and instruments had changed, and the old acoustic piano had been replaced by a donated Baldwin SD-10 concert grand piano. Jim enjoyed worshiping with the Praise Team, while Lauryn worshiped with the congregation. The kids who had been in their children's classes and youth group were Elders and other leaders. Jim thought the pastor preached a fine sermon.

After the worship service, Lauryn and Jim went back to the hotel and relaxed. They told the hotel staff that they would have lunch in their suite, and they asked not to be disturbed. They weren't.

Julie had done her best that evening, and she and Al were gracious hosts for the Presidential fundraiser aboard Long Beach's famous Queen Mary hotel. Casper and Diane Whirry sat with them at the head table, along with Alfred and Julie Wells. The surprise for Lauryn and Jim was the presence of Juliette Debré, who flew in from New York for the weekend. She and Julie were friends by the end of the evening.

Jim gave a short speech, and he talked about how the Whirrys had convinced him to run for governor, but before Jim could decide whether or not to run for re-election, the Whirrys had nominated him to run for President. He then talked briefly about what he had done since getting elected. He had three standing ovations.

That night, they raised more than half again as much as had been raised during the entire previous campaign. By the time Air Force One touched down at Andrews Air Force Base, they were exhausted. It was a productive beginning.

In the early summer, there was another Populist Politics Assembly, and this time it was held in the Fort Worth Convention Center. Paul Wilson kicked things off, and three days later, Jim closed it. The atmosphere there was similar to that of the national conventions for the Democrats and Republicans, but there was no voting. No one attempted to compete with James Smith. In his speech, Jim told the audience what Alfred and Julie Wells had accomplished aboard the Queen Mary.

After returning from Populist Politics Assembly, Lauryn stepped back from being in the public eye as much. She wanted Jim to be in the spotlight with the media. Lauryn made appearances every week or two, but she had other things going on.

Lauryn, Ronnie, and Katheryn Suvari had video conversations nearly every week. Jason Pounds set up a totally secure way for them to bypass phone connections using the Internet for their video calls. The same connection also enabled them to share data files. Different technologies were developed to contain the heat of the first fusion reactor generator. Instead of choosing which technology to use or not use, they ended up using five. With more layers of technology developed, there was a dramatic increase of efficiency.

Before Casper Whirry had married Diane, he had purchased land in the California desert east of Shoshone and just west of the Nevada border. Over a period of several years, he had built a solar power generating array there. From that array, he sold power to Pacific Gas and Electric (PG&E).

As a strictly private project, Casper and Diane decided to utilize the new fusion generating technology to build a plant there. It took more than two years. He notified PG&E that he was ready to supply them a much greater amount of power, both day and night.

Grant Walker, the CEO of PG&E, was given a tour of all but the most secure area of the plant. With him were fourteen of his staff. Casper had given them no indication that the plant was being built. It simply looked like a large warehouse at the edge of Casper's property.

After the tour, they went back to the business offices of Whirry Power. Grant Walker had been shaking his head in wonder for over an hour. "Casper, we've known each other for more than fifteen years. It will take five or six months to increase our ability to receive power from this previously just solar plant. Assuming we hook up this fusion generator to our power grid, how much more power will you be selling to us?"

Casper smiled. "Take a deep breath and let it out, Grant."

"Okay."

Casper looked directly at his old friend. "Believe it or not, the output of the fusion generator can be up to fifteen thousand megawatts."

The mouths of everyone in the room except Casper's hung open. Grant practically shouted. "What? That's more than the output of Grand Coulee Dam in Washington State. Your new plant takes up a fourth of that space or less."

Casper nodded. "About a fifth, actually. Assuming you can use about half of the power I mentioned initially, Diane and I will regain our investments in research and development, along with the construction costs of this plant, in six or seven years, but Diane and I have made arrangements on the Stock Market so that we won't have to wait that long."

Lauryn knew that what was taking place in the California desert was going to go down as a great moment in history. After Lauryn, Ronnie, and Katheryn Suvari watched videos of that desert meeting with Lauryn's staff, Jim and Lauryn invited everyone in the West Wing to the White House theater, including the Joint Chiefs.

After everyone had seen the videos, Jim caught the eye of the Chairman of the Joint Chiefs, General Evan Bradford. Quietly, Jim said, "Evan, let's head downstairs." The Chairman nodded. Ten minutes later, the Situation Room was staffed as usual. After they were seated, Jim spoke quietly. "I've been getting security briefings every day since before I was first sworn into office. The only time

I've heard the phrase "fusion research" used was when there were joint war games in France. I've already talked to our F.B.I. Director in private. Now, I'd like to hear from our C.I.A. Director."

The man was obviously embarrassed. "Mr. President, if you want me to admit that we've been caught flat-footed, okay. We didn't have a clue this was developing. Stan?"

The F.B.I. director shook his head. "It's the same here." They both looked at the President.

Jim smiled. "Good. Lauryn has prepared thumb drives for all of you with the information you need." He handed a box to Evan. "I'll summarize." In just over ten minutes as the thumb drives were passed around, the President told the story from the Johnson Space Center town hall, to the work of Lauryn, Ronnie, and Katheryn, on to Lauryn's breakfast with the Whirrys, and finally on to the present.

The President took a sip of water. "I knew about all of this, but I've kept it under my hat because we could not take the slightest risk of any politician getting wind of this. As I am speaking, word of this new power plant is getting out by word of mouth. The next thing that will undoubtedly happen, will be in the next few days, bills will emerge in both houses of Congress to provide government financing for these new plants. Congress will have competition for that funding, however."

Evan Bradford stared at Jim. "What competition?"

"A stock offering became available almost two years ago called Whirry Holdings. Investors have been able to invest in both this plant and future plants, because the stock's holdings are in the future of power generation."

That evening at dinner, Lauryn and Jim talked about investing in Whirry Holdings. "After you become a former President, Jim, we can invest in it, but by that time the price might be much higher."

"No, my darling, neither of us have ever been greedy. My Presidential pension will be ample, won't it?"

She nodded. "Definitely. If this technology is as good as I think it is, it will gradually replace all the reactors based upon fission within a couple of decades, maybe sooner."

"I agree. Have you talked with Julie Wells today?"

Lauryn shook her head. "Julie and I haven't talked for a couple of weeks. If she hasn't told Al already, I'm sure she will soon. With more and more streaming on the Internet, foreign markets for American entertainment have been gradually becoming less profitable. Julie thinks that Americans and Europeans can work together to produce a wider variety of entertainment than either market offers currently."

"You're probably right. I'll be going to the G-20 Summit next month. Would you like to come along?"

"I'd love to. We have friends in most of those countries. Next week, I have another network luncheon scheduled in New York."

"Good. You might consider planning ahead with your network. See if you can casually find out anything in advance of the Summit that will be helpful to us. By the way, it is likely that both houses will pass a bill to finance construction of more fusion reactors by an overwhelming majority."

Lauryn shook her head. "I seriously doubt that any utility will take advantage of available government financing."

"Why?"

"Do you remember that day when you and I rode on the Tijuana Trolley?"

"Sure! We had a good time, didn't we?"

"Yes, but did you know it was efficiently financed by local banks and why?"

He put his fork down. "It happened when a man named Wilson was mayor of San Diego, wasn't it?"

She nodded. "That mayor was a distant relative of Paul's. He ran for the U.S. Senate and did a good job, but when he ran for President, he didn't succeed."

"Your point?"

"Discussion of a light-rail line from downtown to the border was discussed for years, but it never happened because, with the required federal financing, the city didn't want to raise the taxes that much. The mayor's solution was to produce unique approaches to both financing and construction with the city, the banks, and the unions. The Trolley was built in a fraction of the time and at a fraction of the cost by avoiding federal financing."

"Really!"

Lauryn smiled. "This is why I'm convinced that the utility companies will probably avoid federal financing and build them with private investments. Whirry holdings can provide the needed financial buffer that can make these things happen."

Lauryn was correct. Within less than six months, seven utility companies were starting construction of fusion power plants. Environmentalists tried on several fronts to halt construction, but their efforts failed because they had no evidence to show that the specific design of the fusion reactors was more dangerous than other sources of energy.

During this time, the holidays were approaching. Lauryn and Ronnie worked long hours to arrange for the entire Smith family to be able to celebrate Christmas together at the White House. That was months away, but first Lauryn and Jim would go to the G-20 Summit.

12.
Winding Down

Outside in New York City, it was hot and humid. Inside the United Nations building, however, it was cool and comfortable. Lauryn looked around the room. There was a half-dozen men scattered among nearly seventy women. Ronnie suggested that the luncheon simply be a buffet affair, with a few tables and chairs. Most people were standing.

Lauryn was drinking coffee as she listened to Jillian Wright, the wife of the Ambassador from the United Kingdom, John Cromer. "I think that's about all I dare to tell you, Lauryn. John knows I'm talking with you today, and he wants me to be careful, so we not step on any diplomatic toes."

Lauryn nodded. "I'll pass this on to Jim. He has good diplomatic instincts. We won't embarrass either you or the United Kingdom at the G-20."

"I know, my friend. I trust you. Juliette told me that she needed to speak with you before this luncheon is completed." She gestured. "She's over there near where the chef is carving prime rib."

Lauryn nodded. "I see her. Thank you for the tip." She moved towards the steam table with the hot food and started filling a plate. As the chef was putting thin slices of prime rib on her plate, Juliette looked up and spotted Lauryn.

"Lauryn! Trés bien! It is good to see you!" They hugged.

"It is good to see you too, Juliette!"

The French woman lowered her voice. "Paul told me to tell you that Jim should be extra cautious of Mikhail Rumyantsev. There is intrigue happening within his borders."

"Can you tell me more?" Lauryn kept her voice low.

Juliette shook her head. "I wish I knew more."

"Okay. Thank you for the tip."

Lauryn and Ronnie continued to mix with the others all afternoon. The sun was nearly setting when their helicopter returned to the White House. Ronnie headed off of the White House grounds, but Lauryn saw Jim on the porch and walked towards him.

As they hugged, Lauryn spoke into Jim's ear. "I have something for you that Jay should probably hear."

Jim kissed her. "Okay, let's go into the Oval." As they stepped inside, the President called out. "Jay?"

He came in from his office. "Yes, Mr. President?"

"Lauryn, let's sit down while you tell both of us."

The First Lady carefully laid out for them what she had learned from Jillian and from Juliette. "I didn't prod my two friends because I knew that they would tell me more if they had anything worthwhile."

Jim shook his head. "Our C.I.A. hasn't picked up on any of this. Jay, none of this has appeared in my security briefings."

Jay also shook his head. "As far as I know, none of our intelligence agencies have picked up on this. Mr. President, I think we should discuss this downstairs. Lauryn, you can tell your chef that dinner might be a little later this evening."

"Right." The three of them stood up, and just outside the Oval Office, Lauryn headed towards the residence while the other two went down to the Situation Room. It was only eight days before the G-20 Summit of state leaders in

Rome. There were additional preparations that needed to be made by both the President and the First Lady.

When Air Force One touched down in Rome, the motorcade took Jim and Lauryn to The St. Regis Rome Hotel first. After they were settled into their suite, they only saw one another at formal meals and at night. Lauryn stayed in their suite almost the entire time and received visitors from other countries.

Early on the second day, Lauryn got a call from someone in the Russian delegation, with a translator asking if Lauryn would have lunch with Annette Rumyantsev. The First Lady took the high road. "Certainly, sir. I will arrange for her to join me here at the St. Regis in the private dining room at noon. Will that be satisfactory?" (She had to be polite and respectful.)

"Yes. That will be.... We will escort her there at noon."

"Very well." Lauryn hung up, maintaining the upper hand. She called the front desk and arranged for a small private dining room. Then she called the American delegation's concierge. "I am to have lunch here at the St. Regis with Annette Rumyantsev at noon. Who will be my interpreter?"

"Your interpreter will be Mike Sanders, Mrs. Smith."

"Okay, I would like to talk with Mike beforehand. Will you please send him to our suite as soon as possible?"

"Yes, Mrs. Smith, I will take care of it."

Less than five minutes later, there was a knock on Lauryn's door. The man greeted her with a slight Texas drawl. "Good morning. I'm Mike Sanders. I understand you wanted to see me?"

Lauryn nodded. "Yes, Mike, please come in and sit down." They sat down in a conversation pit near the doors to a large balcony. "Mike, I understand you are going to be my interpreter at a luncheon today at noon here in the hotel. The woman I'm meeting is Annette Rumyantsev."

"Yes! She is somewhat like royalty, descended from an old Russian family. She speaks only a little English. She can be quite pleasant, but since her marriage nine years ago, she has become more – shall we say – hardened."

Lauryn nodded. "I understand. I am concerned that she and her interpreter may use one of the more obscure Russian dialects at least part of the time."

Mike nodded. "So, you have been warned."

"Yes. Mike, I want to be on even footing with them. I am familiar with your linguistic abilities. When I was completing my Ph.D., I had a classmate who spoke another language that you speak." Lauryn began speaking in nearly flawless Navaho. She told Mike that, if Annette and her interpreter start speaking in anything except Standardized Russian, Mike was to translate what they were saying into Navaho.

Mike smiled, and chuckling, he told Lauryn that it would be a pleasure. Then Lauryn would respond in English, which he would translate for them into flawless Russian.

In the little dining room at shortly before noon, Lauryn's interpreter, Mike, sat on her right. Annette's interpreter sat across from him, although Annette spoke English moderately well, briefly. Then she switched to Ukranian, which her interpreter translated into English.

When Mike translated what he said into Navaho, her interpreter became pale, but Lauryn responded in English. "It is a pleasure to meet you as well, Annette. I hope all four of us will enjoy this luncheon, and that we will become friends." Annette's interpreter turned that into Standardized Russian. Lauryn rang a small silver bell beside her water glass, and waiters began serving the luncheon.

As their salads were placed in front of them, Annette said something in the Adyghe language, but before her interpreter could respond, Mike translated it into Navaho and used a secret phrase to tell Lauryn that the others were trying to be deceptive.

Lauryn nodded before responding. "I understand your difficult position. We are both the wives of powerful men trying to be faithful to both our husbands and our countries." Her interpreter translated that into Russian.

During the next hour, Annette tried three other Russian dialects, which Mike promptly translated into Navaho.

When they finished their deserts, Annette said something in Standardized Russian, which Mike translated into English. "She says, she has enjoyed the lunch, and that the next time she hopes her English will be better so that she will not need an interpreter." They said their farewells, and Lauryn gave Annette a hug.

As they got on the elevator, Mike spoke quietly. "I think her interpreter wasn't just frustrated because you and I spoke Navaho. He seemed uncomfortable with some of the things she said. He seemed appalled that she said that she would like to become part of your network."

Lauryn nodded. "It will be interesting to see if the network continues to thrive into the next administration." She left Mike on his floor and continued on to hers.

With great fanfare, they boarded Air Force One after breakfast of the third day. Both Lauryn and President knew it was their last event on foreign soil during his administration. When they landed back at Andrews A.F.B., the calendar said that the election was less than a month away.

On the election night, there were three major candidates running for President. In addition to California Senator Paul Wilson, there was the Governor of New York, a Democrat, and there was a Congresswoman from Texas, a Republican. Paul Wilson had secured the services of Adam Paxton to run his campaign.

On election night, Lauryn and Jim watched the election results until shortly after 9:00 PM, but at that point, there did not appear to be a likely result. They went to bed. The Presidential wake-up call was at 5:00 AM, but Lauryn turned over and went back to sleep. Jim quietly got dressed and headed to the Oval Office.

Jay was there when Jim walked in. "Mr. President, believe it or not, the results were not definite until about an hour ago. It's now definite. Paul won."

"Really! That's great! I was worried that.... No, I won't go there. Paul will make a terrific President, and Dot will be every bit a fine First Lady as my beloved Lauryn. While I'm still here, they have a standing invitation to dinner with Lauryn and me. Between now and January, if they are in town and want to come to the White House, adjust my schedule if you can, to accommodate them, okay?"

"Yes, Mr. President."

Jim's personal cell rang, and he reached into his pocket and looked at the screen. "It's my youngest." Jay went into his own office as Jim touched a button. "Good morning Zack! Did you vote?"

"Good morning, Dad. Yeah, both Judy and I voted by absentee ballot, so we watched the election results for a while. I'm glad Paul Wilson won. He's been a good friend to our family for a long time."

"Yes, he has. Let me connect us to your Mom's phone." He pressed a few buttons on his phone." "Good morning, dear, Zack is on the phone with us. Zack, you mentioned Judy Franz. Your Mom and I have gotten several good laughs over the gossip about you two. We watched her latest movie, *The Crown Prince*, on Friday. We liked it."

"Yes! We sure did, Zack!"

"Yeah, well, I was on the set part of the time as they were shooting it. I'm calling you from Lake Tahoe. Judy and I tied the knot last evening at that little chapel that you and Mom like so much."

"Fantastic! Congratulations, Zack! Can you put her on the speaker with you?" Jim sat down at his desk.

"Yes, Zack, congratulations! Put her on with you!" Lauryn's voice was filled with excitement.

"Good morning, Mr. President! Madam First Lady! This is Judy Granger!"

"Good morning, Judy!"

"Congratulations! You can just call me 'Dad.'"

"Yes, and please call me Mom."

"Okay, Mom! Dad! Zack and I are going to spend a few more days here in Tahoe!"

"Yes, and then we want to come to Washington. Would that be okay?"

"Yes! Yes!" Lauryn was overflowing with excitement. "This is Wednesday. If you get here by Saturday evening, I'll get hold of Tony and Abby, Claudia and Greg, and Brittany and Mason. We can have a family dinner, Judy. Do you have some relatives whom you'd like to join you and Zack for Saturday dinner?"

"Oh, Mom, that would be wonderful! I have a sister in Atlanta, and my parents live in High Point, North Carolina."

The President was leaning back in his chair and relaxing. "Kids, your Mom and I will arrange for suites for all of you at the eDreams hotel, which, as Zack knows, is just down the street from the White House." Jay walked in and beaconed to him. "Listen, duty calls, so I'll ring off and see you next weekend."

"Okay!"

In the residence, Lauryn continued to talk with them for another fifteen minutes or so. She was still in bed. When she hung up with Zack and Judy, she dialed Ronnie. "Good morning, Ronnie! I'm sorry to call you so early, but the

President and I just got off the phone with our youngest, Zack."

"Good morning! What's up?"

"Zack is in Lake Tahoe, where he eloped with Judy Granger last evening."

"Whoa! It's even earlier out there by three hours!"

"Right. My husband went into the Oval Office without breakfast, and that call met him there. How soon are you going to be getting in this morning?"

"I'll be headed out the door in less than ten."

"Good. As soon as you get in, call the White House cafeteria downstairs and have them send up breakfasts for you and me. Order whatever you want for yourself on my tab, and get me a short stack with syrup, bacon, orange juice, and coffee for me. I should be in the office in twenty, okay?"

"Okay, a short stack, bacon, juice, and coffee. I've got it. I'll see you in about twenty." She hung up.

Lauryn got up, kneeled beside the bed to pray, and then headed into her closet. Just over twenty minutes later, her breakfast was waiting on a small table in her office.

Ronnie walked in. "Good morning, again. Our breakfasts got here about a minute ago. They should be hot." They sat down.

Lauryn bowed her head. "Thank you for everything, Father. We love you, and we love Jesus, in whose name we pray, amen." She looked up across the table at Ronnie. "Let's do some brainstorming. Currently, my four kids and their spouses will probably join us for dinner on Saturday. Judy is inviting her sister and parents to join us. You and I will need to get suites reserved at eDreams for at least Saturday and Sunday nights for them. We need to talk to Phil Kaiser about where all of us can go to church on Sunday morning. Another thing I want us to consider is having a wedding reception on Sunday after church."

Ronnie smiled. "And we're going to put all this together in less than five days. This is our kind of challenge!"

Lauryn nodded and ate a forkful of pancakes. "It's a good thing the election is behind us on the calendar. You, I, and the whole staff have a lot to do between now and Saturday afternoon!" She sipped her coffee thoughtfully. "We'll have to limit the size of the reception, assuming we can pull it off."

Ronnie sipped some juice. "Limited to family?"

"We won't invite those in our network for this. We should have an ambassadors' dinner before Christmas. Let's select some of the longest-standing members of the White House Press Corps. We haven't invited the Supreme Court justices since the second inauguration ball, so let's invite them. Let's invite the majority and minority leaders and their spouses of the Senate and House, but not their whips or others. We'll invite Cabinet members and their spouses, and the west wing staff. That's more than enough."

"Okay, Lauryn. When will you be hearing again from Zack and Judy?"

"I don't know for sure. They are going to honeymoon there at Tahoe through Friday, then they will fly out here on Saturday. There's something more that you may need to keep in mind, Ronnie."

"What's that?"

"We don't know about Judy or anyone else coming to this that's from her side of the marriage. If anyone presents us with a security issue, it might be that someone on our staff will have to be an unofficial escort for them for the duration of the reception.

Ronnie smiled. "Our staff seems to thrive on those kinds of interesting challenges. I doubt that would be much of a problem for us."

"I hope you are right." Lauryn swallowed the last of her orange juice. "Today, I want you to find a few minutes to confer with Jay regarding our attendance list for the reception and the excursion to church."

"Okay, I'll take care of it."

13.
Shock and Awe

Saturday's dinner was served to the families around a large round table, that could seat up to twenty. As they were all being seated by the wait staff, Lauryn murmured to Jim, "I'm even more impressed with Judy than I was in the movie last Friday. She's not just photogenic outside. She's beautiful inside as well."

"Agreed." Then he spoke in a normal tone of voice. "Zack, how did you two meet each other?"

"Dad, it was one of those things that only happens in movies." Judy nudged him and put her head on his shoulder briefly. "Do you remember when I went to New Delhi, and I played drums on the praise team for Li Jie when he did that week of evangelism?"

The President nodded. "Sure! That's when your reputation as a professional drummer began to take off."

Zack nodded. "Praise God. Judy was in New Delhi because she was guest starring in a Bollywood movie being made near there."

Judy smiled broadly. "I was not a Christian at that point, but I had heard a lot about the band that was playing during that Li Jie evangelism campaign. As I listened to their first set of music, for some reason, my eyes were drawn to Zack. Subsequently, as I listened to Li Jie preach, I was moved in ways I had never imagined. I went forward and gave my life to Jesus, and then I went back two more nights. On the third night, I told one of my bodyguards that I wanted to meet the band. That's when Zack and I met and became friends. With God's help, we began to run into each other in more places."

Zack leaned over and kissed her cheek. "At first, I had a hard time believing that this woman and I were becoming good friends. Whatever we talk about, it is as though we have known each other all of our lives. A week ago, we went to church together, and at lunch after the worship service, I asked her if she thought of Jesus as her best friend as well as her Savior."

Judy looked at Lauryn. "Mom, I just stared at him as something clicked inside my head. I said, 'Yes, Zack, I know he's my best friend as well as my Savior. Will you marry me?"

Lauryn put her fork down and stared at her new daughter. "So, you asked Zack and not the other way around?"

"Yep! When a woman knows, a woman knows!"

There were exclamations all around the table. Judy's mother, Sophia nodded and smiled. "When Judy was fourteen, I told her that when the right man came around, she would know. She did."

Judy nodded. "Mommie said that to me on my fourteenth birthday."

By the time they had all finished their desserts, it was late. Lauryn and Jim's guests were taken to the eDreams hotel, after they were told that they would be picked up for worship the next morning at 8:40.

Lauryn and Jim had gone to St. John's Episcopal Church once before, but both preferred less ritual when they worshiped. That Sunday morning, three of the Presidential family that worshiped together there said afterward, that they had sensed God's presence that morning. Capitol Police kept the media off of the property, even as the worshippers were drinking coffee and tea in front of the entrance afterward. Many people gathered around Zack and Judy to congratulate them.

Most of them went back to the eDreams Hotel from there because the White House Reception for the newlyweds was not scheduled to start until noon. Judy put her arm through Jim's, on the other side of Lauryn. "Dad, Mom, thank you. I'm saying that not just because of the dinner last night. I know the reception is a big deal, and we may not get a chance to thank you properly later."

Jim squeezed her arm. "You're welcome. We're glad you are our new daughter."

Lauryn looked over at her. "Amen to that!"

There were more people at the reception than Lauryn and Ronnie had planned. The President's body man, Demarcus, secured a live band for those who might want to dance. They started playing after the first hour. The President took the First Lady onto the dance floor, and others began to dance as well.

Judy approached the Presidential couple after the first song and asked if she could dance with The President. "Dad, has Zack told you or Mom about what we're going to be doing over the next three weeks?"

"No. What's happening?"

"I'm to be one of the leads in a Christmas movie that's coming out on the Hallmark Channel the second week of December. Zack has a small part in it too. We'll be flying out to Cleveland early tomorrow morning. Zack told me that the family is going to have a White House Christmas."

"That's right, Judy. If you and Zack want to, I'll arrange for you two to sleep in the Lincoln Bedroom together. Each Christmas, our children vote on who's to sleep there."

Judy squeezed him. "We'll be honored! Will this be Zack's first time?"

"Right." He saw Jay's beacon to him. "Judy, you'll have to excuse me. Duty calls."

"Okay. Thank you, Dad."

It was nearly sunset when most of the people had left. When the band stopped playing, it was over. That evening, Lauryn ate a lite supper with the family, with all of them eating off of trays in the living room. It was a long and tiring day. Lauryn took a long hot shower and went to bed. She was sound asleep when Jim came in.

Lauryn was already in her office when Ronnie came in on Monday morning. "Good morning! We squeezed through with a decent reception, didn't we?"

Ronnie smiled. "Yes. It was especially enjoyable for Jason. The Secret Service had him hang around the bride's sister, Mikayla. When she was a college freshman, she had led a protest against President Stallings and got arrested. From what I observed, I think Jason maybe has a crush on her."

Lauryn had a slight smile. "Really! Mikayla didn't seem like the protester type when I talked with her." Her desk phone rang. The caller ID simply indicated a call from Malibu, California. She picked up the handset. "Hello?"

"Lauryn, this is Diane Whirry. Casper had a heart attack last night. He's gone home."

The First Lady's mouth hung open. "Oh, Diane!"

"I'm numb, Lauryn. He had a complete physical two months ago and was given a clean bill of health. He was four years older than me at 83."

"I don't know what to say, Diane. I'm shocked."

"We all are. I asked to speak to you because I know the President must be busy. Tentatively, there will be viewings and a funeral at Saddleback Church in Lake Forest next Saturday."

"Okay. I'll pass it on to Jim. If we can, we'll be there."

"Thank you. As soon as I can get reorganized, I want to fly to Washington to spend time with you and Ronnie. I'm hoping that next year the two of you can help me complete Casper's pet project he has been working on secretly for the last five years."

"I can only guess about his pet project, Diane."

"I know. I'll tell you all about it when I see you."

"Okay. Even if Jim cannot get away, I'll try to be there with you next Saturday."

"Thank you, Lauryn." They hung up.

She touched a button. "Ronnie, please come back in."

Entering, she came back in and sat down next to Lauryn's desk. "When that call came in, you turned pale. What's happened?"

Lauryn sighed. "Last night, Casper Whirry died of a heart attack."

"No!" She paused, and her eyes were wide. "How old was he?"

"83. The funeral is tentatively set for next Saturday at the main campus of Saddleback Church. I told Diane that, even if the President couldn't make it, that I would try my best to be there."

Ronnie shook her head. "Neither of you can be there. The Ambassadors' Dinner is Saturday night, remember?"

Lauryn's mouth dropped open, and she closed her eyes for a moment. "Of course! This shock has jarred me." She looked up at the ceiling and closed her eyes again, praying silently. Ronnie waited. The First Lady opened her eyes, took a deep breath, and let it out. "I want you to.... Order a single rose and a nice card. I'll write a personal note and enclose a personal check from Jim and me to Saddleback earmarked for evangelism. Send it overnight delivery to the church."

Ronnie was working her phone. "Got it."

"After Paul Wilson is sworn-in in January, Diane wants you and I to help her complete Casper's unfinished pet project. She didn't say on the phone what it is, but I know. This is absolutely just between us, Ronnie."

"Okay."

"For as long as Jim and I have known the Whirrys, they've wanted to come up with a permanent way to dispose of nuclear waste. Just after Jim's first inauguration, Casper conceived of an idea, and it seems to be nearly complete." Lauryn paused. "Have you ever heard of the *Red Force* roller coaster, Ronnie?"

"Sure! It's in Catalonia, Spain. My late husband and I rode on it during our honeymoon. It reaches almost 112 miles per hour in less than five seconds. It's propelled by linear induction, isn't it?"

Lauryn nodded. "You've got the idea. Diane and Casper have property in New Mexico, north of Los Alamos. Under their property, they have dug a tunnel just over two miles long and perfectly straight a thousand feet below the surface at the north end and sloping upward."

Ronnie's mouth hung slightly open. "And?"

At the southern end, the tunnel turns upward to vertical. The opening at the surface is five times the diameter of the tunnel. Now, picture a maglev train engine pushing a car filled with ten thousand metric tons of nuclear waste equipped with booster rockets that ignite after it leaves the tunnel."

Ronnie's eyes got huge. "That's brilliant! Brilliant! If it works!"

"The exit angle at the surface is adjustable by about five degrees. So far, this canon has sent several small payloads to the sun. The whole thing is powered by a fusion reactor that creates chemically pure water from brackish groundwater that is pumped into the Abiquiu Reservoir while the canon is not being used. When small payloads have been shot into the sun, several government agencies suspected other agencies of being responsible for these mysterious rockets that are leaving the Earth. We need to increase the potential payload significantly. Currently, there's more than a hundred metric kilotons of nuclear waste that needs disposal."

"Wow!" Ronnie was visibly impressed. "I'm in if you are!"

Lauryn nodded. "We'll start recruiting any help we'll need on January 21ˢᵗ. Jim and I still haven't decided where we want to live when we move out of the White House."

"You'll want to be close to your kids."

"Yes, but they are a bit scattered. Judy and Zack are still young enough to be flexible. Tony and Abby have already mentioned wanting to retire in the Monterey vicinity of California. Claudia and Greg want to build a log home in the Sierras. If Brittany and Mason decide to live in California as well, that may help Jim and I decide when the family is here at the White House for Christmas."

"Speaking of which…?" Ronnie raised her eyebrows.

"I know. We've been putting off Christmas decorations discussions this year too long. Call your friend at the GSA and ask her to meet with us as soon as possible."

Ronnie stood up. "I'll get on it."

"You do that, and I'm going to call Jay Fillion."

As Ronnie walked out of her office, Lauryn picked up her desk handset and pushed numbers. "Good morning, Jay, this is Lauryn. I got a call from Diane Whirry a while ago. Casper had a heart attack last night and died."

"Oh, no."

"Tell Jim as soon as possible. The funeral will probably be on Saturday at the original campus of Saddleback Church. Because of the Ambassadors' Dinner, neither Jim nor I can go."

"Okay, I tell him right away."

"He'll be shocked, of course."

"Right." They hung up.

Lauryn took out her personal calls phone and returned Diane's call. "Hi, it's me again. I'm so deeply sorry, but Jim and I are hosting the Ambassador's Dinner this Saturday and cannot be with you. If Ronnie and I don't see you before January 21st, we plan to start working on that project as soon as possible afterward, okay?

"Thank you, Lauryn. This means a lot to me. I'll be back in touch with you soon. Thanks again!"

"Of course. I'm grieving with you, my friend! Bye!" They ended the call. The intercom buzzed a few moments later. "Yes?"

"Elyse Johnson from the GSA will be here at 11:00 to discuss Christmas decorations with us."

"Okay. I want Marnette to join us. Her tastes and instincts are congruent with mine."

"I'll tell her."

Lauryn talked with Jim for about fifteen minutes, when he called, as they shared memories of Casper. Lauryn was thankful for Jim's call because she knew that they couldn't get together for lunch.

Elyse Johnson was prompt, and she and Ronnie came into Lauryn's office on the hour. "It's nice to meet you too, Elyse. I see you've brought a tablet with you. By any chance, do you have pictures of White House Christmases past?"

Elyse nodded. "Yes, ma'am. Would you like me to feed images to your video monitor on the wall?"

"Please do. I'm particularly interested in Christmas decorations prior to the Kennedy Administration."

Elyse smiled. "Yes, Ma'am. May I ask why?"

Lauryn started watching the monitor as images began to go by. "I want to base this year's decorations upon what no one living today has seen or remembers seeing, yet I want to innovate with things like LEDs and other contemporary technology."

"That's an excellent approach, Ma'am." Lauryn, Ronnie, and Marnette discussed the old images with Elyse for over an hour. "I understand now, Ma'am. Those two previous administrations created truly spectacular decorations, and we can combine those two themes. I'll have computer-generated images for what I will propose by the day-after tomorrow."

Lauryn stood up. "Excellent, Elyse. I'll look forward to that. Ronnie, set aside a couple of hours for that on my schedule." Ronnie nodded.

Evidently, Elyse and the GSA began putting it all together as the Ambassadors' Dinner approached, took place, and was cleaned up. During the week following the big dinner, Christmas decorations began to appear. The week before Christmas, the White House Press Corps was given permission to explore and report on all that the GSA had come up with. The media were stunned. On the Saturday evening before Christmas, Lauryn provided the media with a personalized tour of the White House Christmas decorations. That video was constantly repeated throughout the networks and the Internet until Christmas.

The day before Christmas Eve, family members got comfortable in their suites at the eDreams Hotel, as snowflakes steadily added to the Capitol's previous white deposits. Christmas Eve and Christmas Day were mostly set aside for those working in the White House and their families, including the Press Corps.

The President's surprise for the First Lady arrived at the White House while the family was having lunch. He announced it while they were eating. "All of you, I think, have heard of a director named Alfred Wells. Does anyone not know who he is?" They all nodded. "He called me the day-after Thanksgiving. He knew of course that I have a lot of musician friends in the entertainment industry. He began calling some of some of them. Right now, a full orchestra is assembling in the ballroom, and they will play the rest of the afternoon and into the evening. Also, Al arranged for the Temple University Concert Choir from Philadelphia to sing for us this evening."

Even Judy was impressed. "Wow! I'm looking forward even more to this. Zack?"

He nodded. "Mom and Dad have some great friends."

Lauryn smiled. "Jim and I really enjoyed your Christmas movie, Judy. We watched it last week. Our dinner tonight will be buffet style. There are people working here 24/7, so each can take advantage of the music and food when convenient anytime between 4:00 and 8:00. Ronnie and I have got things set up so that all the White House staff can have dinner with their families here."

The presidential family stayed through the day after Christmas before heading back to their homes. Lauryn and Jim began to focus more on moving to California's Stanislaus National Forest, northwest of Yosemite. Tony and Abby found a log home for them there. Their home and support buildings would be sitting on two acres of a fifteen-acre parcel. The day after their children left, Lauryn notified the Secret Service and the GSA that she and Jim would be moving there in January.

After watching fireworks going off over the tidal basin on New Year's Eve, Lauryn and Jim shared a bottle of champagne, took a shower, and retired for the evening. Jim did not leave a wake-up call, but he told Jay to have the operator ring him if needed. He wasn't.

The remaining three weeks in the White House seemed to fly by quickly. Several times, Lauryn and Ronnie talked with Katheryn Suvari about Casper's unfinished project. When Lauryn called Ainsley Schafer, the Tours Director Johnson Space Center was excited. "Lauryn! I want to help! I can take a leave of absence here and go New Mexico right away. My late husband and I took escape times off to the Abiquiu Reservoir several times. Diane and Casper Whirry invited us to their home just south of there several times."

"That's great. Ronnie and I plan to fly into Santa Fe sometime during the last week of January. We'll see you then."

Lauryn and the President weren't starting to pack yet, but she was already making plans. She and Jim would fly on Air Force One directly to Sacramento International, and a limo would take them to their new home. The following week, Lauryn would fly to Santa Fe, where she would meet Ronnie, and they would drive to the Whirry estate.

Lauryn and Jim gave gifts to most of the Cabinet members and to Jim and Lauryn's staff members. On January 20th, they spent much of the morning saying their good-byes. While Jim signed pardons, Lauryn sent out a blanket of personal emails to those on her network, reminding each of them of her email address and her social media pages. She hired the secretarial service based in Sacramento that she and Jim had used when he was governor to handle those electronic communications along with her postal mail.

On January 20th, Lauryn sat down at her desk and composed a handwritten letter to Diane Wilson, who would be the next First Lady. She knew that she and Diane would remain close friends. Lauryn also wrote a letter to Tonia Stallings, the previous First Lady. Lauryn told Tonia she wanted to meet her for lunch sometime over the summer. Their retirement home was near Reno, Nevada. He grew up east of there, in Ely.

On January 25th, Diane Whirry arranged for a private jet to fly Lauryn directly to a private airstrip on the Whirry property in New Mexico. Diane flew Ronnie in the following day. Katheryn Suvari and Ainsley Schafer were already there.

Diane led Lauryn on a short tour. "As you know, Lauryn, each load of nuclear waste must reach a final velocity of just over twenty-five thousand miles per hour in order to escape Earth's gravity, eventually to plunge into the sun. Because this train does not have to deal with air resistance while it is in the tunnel, two miles of continuous acceleration got the small payloads to over half the needed velocity before leaving the tunnel. After two miles of acceleration, the train uses multiple braking systems on the remainder of the track as the payload goes ahead and breaks the surface."

Lauryn nodded. "I understand that. Our challenge is to improve the linear induction propulsion and braking."

"Diane smiled. "Exactly. We have more than enough power."

Over the next several months, the four women worked with the five men who designed the system and fifty-six skilled workers to design and implement the improvements that Diane described. Each improvement came with new challenges.

14.
Into the Future

At shortly before midnight on August 17, a five thousand-ton payload was launched with a trajectory so that the sun's gravity would grasp it. Lauryn made a phone call to the Chairman of the Joint Chiefs, General Evan Bradford. "Good morning, General, this is Lauryn Smith."

"Yes, Lauryn, do you know you're calling me on a secure line?"

"Yes, I do. Last night, multiple sources undoubtedly reported an object leaving from northern New Mexico and headed for the sun."

"How do you know about this?"

"That's why I'm calling, General. Last night's launch, along with the previous smaller launches over the last several months, were all part of a private effort started by Casper Whirry before he died in December."

"Go on."

"Although what was detected leaving the Earth was propelled by disposable rocket engines, what was seen was launched by an underground canon. The Whirry property is just south of the Abiquiu Reservoir, as you probably know already. If you and the Joint Chiefs will land on the private air strip on the Whirry property a week from today, please bring with you five thousand tons total weight of nuclear waste properly encased in lead."

"Five thousand tons? You've got to be kidding! I'll just fly out there today myself."

"General Bradford, if you come by yourself, you will of course be welcome. Your pilot can wait in the terminal building. Thus far, no laws have been broken, and this is private property. If the military tries to take over this installation by force, the canon will be sadly but completely destroyed. The security system is first rate, and any individual or group can be detected from miles away."

There was a long pause. "I will confer with President Wilson. If he says yes, I will fly there by myself and land there tomorrow morning before noon."

"As you wish, General." Lauryn hung up.

Diane, Ronnie, and the rest of the design team were listening on wireless earbuds. Diane was smiling broadly. "Whatever happens tomorrow and afterward, the dream that Casper and I have had is fulfilled. Lauryn, what do you think the President will say? You know him pretty well."

She nodded. "Jim and I have known the Wilsons for nearly twenty years. I doubt that there will be a problem."

There wasn't. After the plane landed, General Bradford was led into the Whirry home. Diane greeted him warmly. "Good morning, General Bradford. You and I met previously two years ago, when one of our fusion reactors went online for the first time." She turned to Lauryn. "You two know each other quite well, and you're one of the experts. Why don't you explain how the canon works for General Bradford?"

Lauryn nodded. "I'll show you on this wall monitor first, and then I'll take you to the installation." It took her less than a half hour to give the history of Casper's dream, her own involvement, and what the team had been doing since January. "Now, Evan, I'll give you the tour, though we won't walk the length of the canon." She went to a wall and touched a hidden button. A sliding door opened, and Lauryn, Diane, and General Bradford got on an elevator.

They descended roughly twelve stories before coming to a stop. Diane silently watched as Lauryn first pointed out the freight elevator that brings down the loads. It took less than ten minutes to show him that end of the canon. "Now, we'll get on this sled. Fasten your seat belt, Evan. We will be going only a fraction as fast as the maglev train, but we'll be going fast nonetheless."

At the other end, the sled adjusted the angle in which its passengers were riding as it rose more steeply on the tracks. Finally, the sled came to a stop in the bright New Mexico sunshine. The tunnel's opening was about forty feet below the rest of the desert. "The sled is held here by magnetic brakes because the cargo units are launched at the end of the rails, the tunnel doors close, and the rockets fire."

The general no longer held his cool. "This has been amazing. I've seen it, but it is still unbelievable." He turned his head. "Diane, I only met Casper that once, but evidently he was a man with a vision."

With a half-smile, Diane nodded. "Yes, he was. Lauryn, do you want to tell him about aiming?"

"Certainly. You undoubtedly noticed that the tunnel is seven meters in diameter, but here at the opening, it is much larger. This end of the tracks can be moved in any direction under computer control. The system can adjust the aim of the canon by several degrees right up to the moment of a launch. Now, we'll go back to the other end."

The sled accelerated to nearly two hundred miles per hour before slowing to a stop. "Evan, let's go upstairs and talk." The general accepted Diane's invitation to lunch, and then he flew back to Washington. After watching him take off, Lauryn took out her phone. "Jim, everything went as anticipated. How are things going there?"

"Tony and Abby had everything arranged the way you and I like it, right?"

"Yes, my love."

"How much longer do you think you'll be down there?"

"If the Joint Chiefs come with a payload next week, I'll fly home right after it is launched."

"Wonderful. I've invited Al and Julie Wells to come up here a week from Friday. I assume you'll be back by then."

"I should be, Jim. I'm looking forward to reconnecting with friends from our pre-politics days when we were first married."

"I'm looking forward to that too. This property is so beautiful. I think we'll be entertaining lots of guests."

"I don't think we'll ever have any financial difficulties, Jim."

"Why, has something changed?"

"Diane told me a little while ago about something Casper did while you were president."

"Really!"

"He established a blind trust, and every month he and Diane have deposited shares of Whirry Holdings into the trust. In turn, the trust is part of our living will. Whirry Holdings finances most of the fusion reactors as loans to the utility companies. The canon was also built with money from Whirry Holdings. That stock has soared in value far more than Microsoft."

Other Books by James J. Stewart
Available on Amazon

Christian Inspiration, Study, and Poetry

Faith and Yosemite:
Fourth Edition
[Christian poetry with
pictures of Yosemite]

Faith Fuel
[Meditations on the
Christian faith and life]

Lasting Love
[Short Biographical Sketches]

Living for Jesus
[A Gospels Study Guide for
Couples and Small Groups]

Deliberately
Growing Spiritually
[A five-year Bible reading
program for spiritual
transformation.]

Seed Thoughts for
Christian Prayer
and Meditation
[Workbook]

Single Sentence
Sermons
[Workbook for growing faith]

Walking in Faith
[Much of the same poetry as
Faith and Yosemite but
without pictures]

Spiritually Growing
Through Prayer
The focus is upon personal piety
and spiritual growth through
prayer.

In Jesus' Name
[Praying Effectively]

Christian Fiction

A Man, A Woman
and a Cat
[A cheetah/Puma crossbreed
brings together an architect
and a famous actress.]

A Marriage
of Miracles
[God sets up a whirlwind
romance & fills two people's
lives with miracles]

The Camera Doctors
[Two people meet on top a
famous mountain, and
romance ensues.]

Casting Lots
[Christian romance and

adventure set in the near
future]

Christian Romances
in the Foothills
An anthology of Tom's Town,
Soul Mates, &
The Camera Doctors

An Extensive Life
[The life story of a man who
lived more than
four hundred years.]

Empty Tomb,
Full Hearts
[A Selection of Testimonies
Among Those Who Saw
the Risen Christ]

The Gaardian Saga
[Christian science fiction fantasy involving God in a major role.]

God, Love, and Stargazing
God prepares two people for both romance and divine service.

A Nation Transformed
[A future tale of God intervening in the USA with miracles.

A Second Call to Serve
[A tenth-generation pastor and his second wife accept a call to build a church from scratch.]

Prayer Warriors
[Urban adventures in a near-future continuation of Casting Lots]

Soul Mates
[Romance, the same setting as Tom's Town]

This World Is Not My Home
[Two together since high school separate to find love with others.]

Tom's Town
[Small town life and Christian romance]

The Warrior and the Prophet
[God has surprises and blessings for newlyweds]

Yosemite Picture Books

Ever-Changing Yosemite Valley
[Yosemite Valley is a glacially carved valley. Moment by moment, scenes change.]

Faith and Yosemite 4th Edition
[Pictures of Yosemite, w/ poems about Christianity]

Portraits of El Capitan
[El Capitan rises 3000 feet above Yosemite Valley]

Portraits of Half Dome
[Half Dome marks the east end of Yosemite Valley]

A Sense of Wonder: Yosemite
[A Christian poem, illustrated with pictures]

Starlight Over Yosemite
[Large pictures of Yosemite taken at night]

Yosemite Textures and Shadows
[Photographs of Yosemite depicting all seasons, both day and night]

www.ingramcontent.com/pod-product-compliance
Lightning Source LLC
Chambersburg PA
CBHW070336130626
46556CB00007B/2885